ELIZABETH BAINES was born in South Wales and lives in Manchester. She has been a teacher and is an occasional actor as well as the prize-winning author of plays for radio and stage, and of two novels, *The Birth Machine* and *Body Cuts*. Her award-winning short stories have been published widely in magazines and anthologies. Her first story collection, *Balancing on the Edge of the World*, was published by Salt in 2007. A new novel, *Too Many Magpies*, was published by Salt in 2009.

USED TO BE

By the same author

USED TO BE

Elizabeth Baines

CROMER

PUBLISHED BY SALT

12 Norwich Road, Cromer, Norfolk NR27 0AX United Kingdom

© Elizabeth Baines, 2015

Printed in Great Britain by Clays Ltd, St Ives plc

Typeset in Sabon 10/13

ISBN 978 1 78463 036 2 paperback

1 3 5 7 9 8 6 4 2

for John

CONTENTS

WHAT WAS, WHAT IS

USED TO BE

I'M HOLDING MY seat with both hands here, we're hurtling along the motorway, nose to tail, towards the set of a student film we've both agreed to be in, Sally's giving me a lift and no way is she driving with concentration, she's laughing her head off, she's telling me a story, how she spent a year in Lanzarotte. What a life, she says, My God, life-a-Riley, fantastic cheap food, drinks in the bar all day long, I only came back because I got fat, you wouldn't think it, would you, I used to be fat? No you wouldn't, just look at her, stomach flat as a teenage anorexic's, on show in her hipster micro-mini, schoolgirl hair down her back, you'd never know she was forty, though that's what she's playing in the film because nowadays all the heroes and goodies must look as though they never had a past.

Well also, she says, laughing, we'd outstayed our visas, though but actually we outstayed them ages before, but the cops, see, they were our mates, once a week they rounded us up and stuck us in the cell for an hour and then came for a drink! And she gives a loud crack: whenever she laughs she throws her head back – eyes off the road – and when she talks she always shouts; and now she flings her skinny bare arm out, she's driving one-handed, and in the hand she's flailing she's holding a nut bar, she's eating too.

She slides me a look – my grip tightens – her wide mouth pursed now over a grin, maybe she thinks I'm shocked by the visa-dodging story, or maybe that's just the way her mouth happens to close on her teeth: I didn't know then – it wasn't exactly my priority – and I don't know now, now I'm writing it down.

I used to be a writer who decided for her characters what they were thinking. But something happened, call it age or call it time or call it all the stuff that's happening now in the world. I used to write in measured sentences but now mostly I haven't the patience, not now the world is running away with us, I used to hide behind the third person, but I'm admitting it now, that was me, this is me, clinging onto my seat while she guns us along and yatters: maybe she's just oblivious, she's onto another story now. She'll miss the exit, she's done it both times before, however soon beforehand I warn her, and while she's off in the world of her story the car in front zooms closer and the dial on the clock nudges ninety, and my life as well as the road begins rushing by.

You wouldn't believe it, she is saying, This morning, broad daylight, we had the front door to our flats kicked in, we heard this banging and then this splintering! And I'm seeing the crackhead, which she says he was, which he must be, the way things are now, kicking the door in the brilliant summer morning, her boyfriend running down through the shadowed corridors to accost him, and yet my past life is flashing, a memory gleaming of bright-green marsh all around me, I was six, I had gone to pick a flower, a bright-red flower; somehow, oblivious, I'd found my way without sinking, and then all of a sudden I was trapped by water and lethal green moss on all sides . . .

But the images of her story are also unfolding: the small rundown front garden, the gate which doesn't fit banging on the gatepost as the boyfriend ejects the crackhead, and all the leaves on the trees in that street glittering in the morning sun. And there in bright sunshine too are the motorway barriers whipping beside us, and in my head also the image of the film set we're driving towards: a small suburban semi, a white plastic door with stained-glass roses; and, since we might not make it the way things are going, the image of us arriving if we do; and the story of the film, a young woman violently attacked, and the characters we're playing – me a loud-mouthed factory-worker neighbour, and her the girl's calm and sensible mother – which we'll have to believe in and make real, and with a bit of luck will. And up above, a plane, small and bright in the late afternoon sky, going down towards the airport but seeming suspended because of the speed we're doing, and therefore unreal, an uncertain symbol now that what has happened has happened, bright-coloured, I'd say it looked like a toy, but I no longer trust metaphors, now it's so hard to know what things mean. And all the while, out of sequence, the images from my own life are flicking.

I used to believe in plots, but they're too insistent and simple; there's no such thing as a single setting or a stable scenario, they're always an author's lie.

It's terrible, shouts Sally, it's awful round our way now, it's getting dead rough – and pictures come to me of the time I once happened to live there: the elder tree in my garden which I took as a metaphor for the life I had then, single-parent and lefty: a tree from old wives' tales, ie the tales of independent women, with magical or medicinal properties, with flat creamy blossoms which I said to myself at the time were like sacrament plates. I was hopeful, I was tough and brave. And the image of the spider plant sweeping down from my mantelpiece with all its optimistic vegetative spider-plant babies; and then the image of it smashed: I threw it at my married lover, I wasn't tough, I wasn't brave, I wept and despaired.

And flashing past with the bridges are all my selves: the single mother, the hippy student, the middle-class housewife giving dinners, the teacher's-pet swot, the efficient no-nonsense young professional. And the victim: the young woman put down by her macho male boss, the child the boys threw stones at, flicked school-dinner custard to land in her hair. And then a memory popping up to surprise and shame me: the day I lay in wait with my sister for two girls from the slums and taunted them all the way to school and pulled their hair. The bully.

You should see it at night now, yells Sally, her voice scandalized but also filled with relish, and a sign comes up, we're halfway there, at least we've made it halfway there, to the tiny hall beyond the plastic door, and the two student director-producers in their jeans, and the intent cameraman with his cowboy gait who has a problem, in that cramped kitchen, with camera angles. And I take my eyes off the road and look out at the fields, a flat plain reclaimed from the sea, and my recurring nightmare comes to me, the dream of flooding I've had since a child, the sea surging inland or slipping round, insidious, sly, and very soon the deadly silver stretching to the horizon all round. I used to think it was insecurity, but

6

maybe it was a premonition, the way the world is going. Or maybe it was telling me that, in spite of what narrative so often tells us, nothing, including our personalities, is stable, but fluid.

Sally rubs her nose· takes the hand still holding the nut bar and puts the heel of it on her nose and vigorously wiggles, and I tense, she has to be obscuring her view. She takes it away again – I relax just a little – she says, garrulous, Excuse me, I'm not being rude, I have to do that, I have trouble breathing – I tense again – My nose got broken, I was badly beaten up last year. My jaw as well, she says, I had to have it set, I don't want to talk about any of it, though. And she's already onto something else and laughing. Maybe she was lying, maybe it's just the tyranny of stories, the way they take you over with their own internal logic and their pull towards drama, you say one thing and the story turns it into something else.

Yet the scene comes to me vividly: the dark suburb she says is dangerous now, the muggers huddled in hoodies and Sally approaching, vulnerable, with her naked legs and arms . . . But my own life's still unspooling, and I'm hearing a sound from a day when my marriage was failing, I took the pushchair to the park, a winter afternoon and going dark already, and the sound was the sound of ducks landing on the pond, a sound of slicing, or tearing, I heard it then as a symbol for what was happening to my marriage, a central symbol in a story of ending, mine. Which would only be one story because then I got happy, but I have to say I can't hear ducks landing on water without that particular story coming to the surface and its sadness sweeping me again.

Sally's scrabbling in the pocket – she's finished her nut

bar – someone hoots, we must have swerved; she pulls out a pair of sunspecs, white with a little strawberry to echo the big one on her tiny T-shirt, she says, I love sunpsecs, I've got eight pairs, all different colours! It's like bras and pants, she tells me, I have to match them, which is why I wear a different bra every day. And she laughs. She's put the specs on now, they're like a child's specs, she looks about ten. I'm in danger of constructing a character now: I'm not privy to how she's feeling but I can't help thinking she's just not a serious person.

We miss the exit. And this time we miss the next one, the last one off before the bridge across the river south, there's no choice but to cross it and then turn around. On the bridge there are road works: we hit the build-up and she leans on the brakes. Now we're crawling.

My life has stopped flying by me, the past sinks back; the bright bollards, the glittering cars, the high-up bridge girders, take on a vivid, pressing presence. I have room to think of being irritated – I told her once again to get ready for the exit, once again she didn't – there's a potential drama between us now, me being annoyed and maybe trying not to show it, but I don't know if I am, I no longer even know if I'm a person who gets annoyed about such a thing, and I wouldn't like to say how she'd feel if I did. We're practically standing and the queue stretches ahead right across the half-mile bridge. We have to call to say we'll be late for filming.

Of course she tells me many stories, laughing, as we crawl to the other side, about Lanzarotte, about the band she sings in, about where she shops for clothes and what this outrageous shop assistant said. Trying to turn back we get lost on a ring-road freeway; we take a turn towards the south and I fail for several miles to persuade her to turn back again. We inch back across the bridge. This is the turning, I tell her, but she misses it, and we have to take another, a long way round. We get lost in the town. This is it, I say, this is the way we went the both times before. No, it's not, she says, and drives on and round and round.

At last we're there. She laughs in delight as she pulls up. She breezes before me through the plastic door with roses, and they're all waiting, the other actors, the directors and the film crew: My god, we got lost! She's regaling them, entertaining them, with our adventure, our story, what a hoot, and what a menace those road signs, really confusing, and those roadworks, shouldn't be allowed in rush hour: all scandalized relish and laughter.

It's night filming we're doing. It's dark now. Here we are, dressed for the characters we're playing, me in my factory overall, her in a housewife's apron. We've been waiting for hours while they set up the shoot for this scene, this construct, in which we find the girl, the daughter of the character Sally is playing, who's been violently attacked.

The clock has eased into the early hours. We're exhausted, so tired we don't need make-up after all to make us look our haggard parts.

She's petulant suddenly, stroppy; she says, If this was an Equity job we could demand time and a half.

She says, drama-queen peevish, This scene is really difficult.

Then, as if she realizes she's overstepped it: I think it's

really important, this film, I think it's wonderful they're making it – and now she sounds pious and even precious.

Stripped of her make-up she looks more her age, I've noticed, yet there's something more childlike in her bluish unadorned skin.

And then I see that her nose and eyes are red with unshed tears.

She sees that I've seen. She says, OK, I'll tell you.

Tell me what?

Who it was beat me up last year.

She says, My last boyfriend, the guy I went to Lanzarotte with.

She says, That's who I thought the crackhead was this morning, I thought he'd found where I live.

And there it was, a different plot about Sally from the one I had after all been constructing (plots as refuge, plots as traps). And which still has been working itself out as I've written, pushing up its fear and sadness, and making me remember some scenes from my own life better than others which flashed before me on the motorway that day . . .

But then she rallied and dried her eyes, and the studious-looking young actor playing the hoodie came in wearing his costume, amazingly transformed, and she gave a loud cracking laugh.

THAT TURBULENT STILLNESS

THE TROUBLE WAS – I can tell you – she was prone to taking her cues from Brontë heroines.

I know very well what happened. When she first caught sight of Kevin Flanagan in his black bomber, sauntering along the towpath towards her and Pam, a hole was punched in the bright suburban day, and also in her heart. That's how it felt.

They were just by the cemetery. On the left, from between the tall trees and the looming mausoleums, came a ferny scent of death like a challenge. On the right, the water gelled as if changing chemical composition.

Ahead, Kevin Flanagan's white cigarette arced.

Everyone at school had told them: the Flanagans were tinkers, or had been, before Kevin Flanagan's father fetched up one day in this north-Midlands market town and something about its calm grey square and its church like a frosted cathedral basking in a hollow – or maybe debt, or a feud, who knows? – prompted him to stop moving and settle. He still plied his trade, selling something, nuts and bolts perhaps, his old caravan parked up as an office in the family's back yard in the part of town where tiny brick terraces ran down narrow cobbled streets. Kevin Flanagan was the eldest of several children.

He wasn't tall; he was stocky but slim, powerful-looking,

with strong features that scowled from under a forelock of reddish-brown hair. She'd seen him once or twice with other lads on a street corner when she and Pam had juddered on their bikes down the cobbles, and once at the back of the cinema queue. Each time, in spite of her private school, her parents with their company cars and the big detached home on the wide North Road, she recognised Kevin Flanagan as a fellow spirit.

He reached them on the towpath. He broke from his frown into a grin, his eye-tooth gleaming, and the hole in her chest punched wider.

They got talking. He leaned on the cemetery wall, one foot up behind him.

The trouble was, it was Pam he seemed to want to talk to, Pam who didn't wear glasses and whose mini-skirts were shorter; it was Pam he offered a drag on his fag.

She watched Pam taking it, her little finger crooked. A silence had fallen and she was aware of Kevin Flanagan staring at Pam too as she inhaled dramatically, eyes closed, lids flickering and sheeny.

Nearby, on the railway bridge over the canal, the rails began to hum: beyond the edge of the town the Flying Scotsman was approaching.

Kevin Flanagan broke the spell. 'Come on! Let's get under the girders!'

It's what the local lads did: swing themselves up to lie in a narrow gap at the top of the concrete pillar supporting the bridge, inches from the monster pounding above.

'You're joking!' said Pam, but *she* said, 'OK!' and they

were running, the two of them, her and Kevin Flanagan, they were under the bridge – the rails were ringing now, you could hear the engine thundering – and he was levering himself up, big thighs flexing, then reaching down from his horizontal position to hand her up after him, and just as the engine exploded onto the bridge, his huge hands clamped her to his side.

And the train detonated over them, juddering the girders, vibrating the concrete, thundering through her organs, her blood, filling her ears with a noise so loud it swelled to a kind of silence. On and on – all twelve or so carriages – and there in the whirlwind of noise and vibration she became aware of his body beside her, the swell of his thigh against her own, his big spatulate hands lying now on his hard flat belly, his exotic sharp-musty smell. And in that clamouring silence, in that turbulent stillness, all the middle-class caution of home and school was pounded away.

The last carriage left the bridge, the noise snapped off like a shutter; real silence floated in. They leaned up on their elbows, embarrassed now to be so close to each other's bodies, and she began to lever herself down.

Her body felt weightless.

Pam, waiting below in her pastel clothes, looked domestic, like a puppet, and she knew in that moment that she wouldn't be going around with her much any more.

Just before she jumped, he swung his legs to follow down behind her and his knees caught her shoulders.

She thought of him as her Heathcliff, of course.

Her father hated him, as he was bound to.

In what dubious dealings was Kevin Flanagan's father involved? he wanted to know. Where had he come from? Why did nobody know?

She rolled her skirt higher at the waist, she checked on her birds'-nest hairstyle and left her father with questions dropping round him unanswered, unanswerable, like crumpled false starts on paper.

Even Kevin, who'd been a baby when they settled here, didn't know the answers. Not that she asked him. What she loved was precisely the not knowing, the history wiped, she and Kevin new-born into a brand-new story in which he was the only hero and she the only heroine.

He started work at the paper mill. He bought a motorbike secondhand from a friend and, against her father's strict injunction, she hopped on the back. He kicked the starter, his eye-tooth gleaming, and they roared away from the placid square, the closed shops with their lowered eyes, the church encrusted with history, sending up dry suburban leaves in whorls, making for the moors at the top of the Pennines, for the scouring heather and the wide possibilities of empty sky.

Though as they sat in the heather he'd stare away at the undulating surface, his face half-hidden beneath his tawny forelock, his full lips drawn down at the corners. He was broody and silent, but then he never talked much anyway, and though in these moments she was disappointed by his distance she loved his inchoate passion, so like her own.

She left school. She left the home of her despairing parents to live with Kevin Flanagan in a one-room flat above the Co-op in the market square, approached from an alleyway at the back. She got a job in the gift shop. She laughed at her parents' protestations that if she wanted to be free and avoid a life of small-town bourgeois values, then selling overpriced tat for a minimum wage was hardly the way. They missed the point: that if you lived a life of passion, then working in a gift shop hardly defined you; that if you lived a life of passion, nothing else mattered.

She had brought her books, her shelf of novels, but what mattered was *life*: those moments when, back from work first, she'd look out at the square and see Kevin weaving his motorbike across it towards her, when his key turned in the lock and there was his leather-clad form, silhouetted in a blare of afternoon sun.

Of course, because of their passionate natures they quarrelled – about nothing, things she couldn't afterwards remember, or because when he came home late she felt jealous of the time he'd spent with his mates and with strangers, in garages or pubs, wheeling and dealing. But as they yelled at each other over the room, as he threw down his keys in exasperation, the athletic curve from his straight shoulder to his large loose hand, the tight flex of his leather thighs, the whole air he'd brought back of other worlds out there waiting, would break her resolve, and she'd rush to him, and he would melt too, his wired limbs becoming fluid, and they'd fall into bed, fusing together. *I am Kevin*, she would think, *and he is me*.

It was ridiculous that she should feel jealous. He was doing it for her, for their future together. He had so many plans. Already he had a foot in several businesses. He was working now for a building firm and there was talk of his being taken into the partnership; along with the partners, he had a share in a Sheffield nightclub. The idea of a pizza takeaway – and in the future, a nationwide chain – was in the air.

All her parents' predictions were proving wrong.

'We're going places, you and I,' he told her, pushing her back on the pillows, his torso silky in the lamplight. Outside in the square the town hall clock struck the hour, and she thought of the sound pooling over the town, rippling in circles out over the villages and on to the dark wild hills.

She was buying tomatoes in the market one Saturday when someone said her name. She looked up and there beside her was Trevor Sugden. In the private school, Trevor Sugden had fancied her – no, he'd been *sweet on her*, that was the more appropriate old-fashioned phrase. He was an old-fashioned boy, who would stare at her intently through his horn-rimmed glasses, his pupils brimming with admiration, or love, or whatever it was she didn't like to think of him feeling for her. He had made her squirm.

He'd been away at university, and she hadn't seen him now for about two years.

She stared. It had to be said that he looked more presentable now: his jeans had a tighter, trendier cut, and his windcheater jacket was at least half-decent. There were the eyes, still brimming but steadier now, enough for her not to cut him dead but to say, 'Hey, Trev, how y'doin'?'

Calling him *Trev*, of course, was cruel. It sounded sarcastic, he was definitely a *Trevor*, never a *Trev*. And sarcastic was how she felt, or rather, no, something more subtle: a kind of pitying thrill at her own escape from everything he stood for. She wanted to prolong the sensation; she said, 'I'm going for a coffee. D'you want to join me?'

He followed her between the market stalls to the café – he didn't shuffle or drag obsequiously behind as she might have expected, but she could feel him respectfully letting her lead the way.

They sat in the window.

She told him straight away where she was living, and that she was living with a boyfriend, pointing over the market awnings to the window of the flat and its secretively gleaming panes. As he glanced at it and nodded, she saw how deliberately he kept a bland expression on his face, and she did then feel compunction. He told her about his studies, and the city he was studying in. She was a little surprised by the quietly confident air with which he spoke about it all, and by the way, when the waiter brought him the wrong coffee, he got the matter put right, cheerful and matter-of-fact. He was home for the Easter holidays, he told her, helping his father who ran the furniture business settle into new premises in the town. A prime site it was, he said, just off the market square.

He was clearly ready to tell her all about it. She looked away, impatient.

He said, intent and apparently oblivious to the fact that he was being discouraged: 'It wasn't easy securing it. There were others interested.'

She looked out of the window.

'In the end it all came down to a vote on the Council. And really, if it hadn't been for Councillor Irwin . . . '

She thought: Trust Trevor Sugden to go to university and

end up entangled in small-town politics. She stopped him right there.

She stood up. She hadn't even finished her coffee.

She said, 'I have to get back. Kevin will be getting home.'

'Kevin?'

'Yes, Kevin Flanagan. You know him . . . '

Of course, everyone knew Kevin Flanagan. She watched Trevor's eyes widen, his cheeks colour. Of course, wild, romantic handsome Kevin Flanagan, against whom no nerdy ex-grammar-school boy would ever stand a chance.

Kevin was hunched at the table as she entered.

Something was wrong.

His fists were clenched.

She put the tomatoes on the table and they lay before him, greasily pregnant in their plastic. 'What's the matter?'

He'd been home a while. He said, 'I saw you from the window, going into the café with that bastard!'

She laughed. The word was so inappropriate for someone quite so ineffectual as Trevor Sugden, but also she was shocked, that Kevin should have so little faith in her, so little faith in himself, shocked at the very idea, so alien to what they had between them, that she'd be tempted by anyone else at all, let alone Trevor Sugden. But also she was touched by the strength of his passion.

She put her hands on his clenched shoulders. She turned him towards her, laughing at the ridiculousness of his assumption, and felt him relax.

She thought she had reassured him.

Two days later the police came.

The previous evening, along with a mate, he had sought out Trevor Sugden who was stacking boxes alone in his father's new premises, and they'd given him a beating that had put him in the hospital on a life-support machine.

She lay awake that night, images blossoming like bruises: his head bowed, as they charged him, the droop of his forelock; his leather back view as they led him away. The images she tried to squeeze away: bandages and harsh hospital lights, the bleeping of medical machines . . .

The night felt hollow, a deep crevasse into which their passion had fallen and was rolling, bloodied with violence.

'Come home,' her mother said on the phone.

She was at the window. The mid-week traders were packing up their stalls. Boxes lay around, flattened cardboard was stacked in piles for the bin men, paper flapped around the feet of the scaffolds.

She thought, yes, she might go.

She remembered his head cocked away as they charged him, as if he didn't want to face what he'd done, his shoulders held straight as they led him down the stairs, as if in a bid to withstand himself.

The way that, out of shame, he didn't meet her eye.

Outside, a piece of paper unlocked itself from a metal pole, skidded over the flagstones and became airborne, rising high above the awnings, and up to the roofs and over, towards the prison.

She thought of him in his cell. She saw him lift his head, the forelock sliding. She imagined him mouthing her name.

It was as if, like Jane Eyre, she heard him calling, her lover lost in the darkness of his passion.

'No,' she said to her mother, 'I won't come home.'

Though she couldn't, in all conscience, ignore Trevor Sugden.

Daffodils shivered on the hospital lawn; her feet made an icy crushing sound on the gravel drive.

As she entered his room, Trevor Sugden was easing himself gingerly onto his bed. Plaster and wadding covered his nose. Three weeks after the attack, the bruises on his face were circled with yellow.

He didn't speak. He gestured to the chair.

She said, 'Trevor, I'm so sorry.'

His voice was nasal and thick through the dressings. 'It isn't your fault.' He sighed. 'To some extent, I have myself to blame.'

She said, 'No –' but he went on: 'I should have locked the door. It's not as if we hadn't been warned. We got the Council vote, but those pizza-takeaway guys, they weren't going to give up. They'd broken the window already. They were out to frighten us off.'

She gasped, 'Kevin, you've got it wrong!'

Over the ridiculous dressing, he was looking at her steadily. 'He warned me himself. He came up to the old premises the day before we moved.'

He sighed. 'I could kind of see his point. He said: "You middle-class bastards with your friends on the Council." And he gave me a pretty clear warning; he said: "You and your fucking father won't be getting in my way, mate." '

The word – *mate* – came out like a cough, and Trevor winced over his broken ribs.

So, Reader, she didn't marry Kevin Flanagan. She. I. I didn't marry him. Now, these years later, I see her, my former self, as another person, the heroine, like Cathy, only of a story within a story. And like Cathy's housekeeper Nelly Dean, I watch her from out of a bigger, wider story, and sigh and smile . . .

LOOKING FOR THE CASTLE

You were still miles from home, but the moment of getting there was in your head already, the click of the key in the door, the clang of saucepans from the kitchen, your husband cooking. The sound of things knocking into place. Your life. You put your foot down; the land wheeled, flat as a canvas, a black scribble of petroleum works sliding by in the distance, a contusion of clouds pushing up on the horizon.

And then the sign came up, the name of the town where you lived for two or three years as a child.

You'd never been back, but now the place scraped on your mind: a knot of tanneries and terraced houses in a curve above the watery spaces where the Mersey joins the Manchester Ship Canal, surrounded by green country on the other two sides. The moan of boats coming in from the misty Irish Sea. The black scar of the terrace you lived in. The boom of your father's Irish voice.

The count-down signs to the slip road appeared, and though you didn't intend to, you flicked the indicator, and there you were, driving back towards the memory: the yard of scorched cinders beside the end-terrace house, the high board fence your father erected to keep away prying eyes, a fag stuck to his lip, his big stiff body bending and stretching, the hammer biting and snapping all day. The way, when you went to call him for his tea, his face in answer was cold and impassive, his mouth a hard line. The way you cringed.

The door he made in the side of the fence, the pain and shame leaking out as you and your sister, escaping, stepped through. The cold feel of her fluffy coat, the way she winced as you took her arm.

The walk down the hill, the road unstable-feeling under your feet. The fat woman on her doorstep, arms folded, who stared at you frankly; the kids you didn't know sending calls like radar, missiling past. The turn at the bottom where the Bridgewater Canal plunged beside the road into the scab-red wall of the tannery, an unlit tunnel hammering with factory sounds, slamming with cars.

You stood steeling yourselves as cars batted past, teetered at the entrance on the narrowest of pavements, hit by your own flapping clothes. In a gap in the traffic you held your breath and grabbed hands, and ran like mad to the other side.

The other side, where the industry ended and another landscape began: a double row of pink semi-detached houses lacing up a steep hill between fields, and at the top an ancient village with a ruined castle: an escape to a fairytale land.

Now, all these years later, you were on a ring road that didn't exist then. You couldn't see the town, hidden by curtains of newly planted trees, and you didn't recognise the district names on the signs. At last a name seemed vaguely familiar, but when you turned off, the view opening up was nothing like the dark clotted place you'd remembered: ahead, beyond a small park, pale modern industrial roofs tipped away to the river in the distance. As you turned at the junction you saw the glint of the nearby canal, and a short way along, a sign with the name of the road where you lived.

The whole area was razed. The factory had gone, the ground where it stood landscaped over. No one would know it had ever been there.

⬥

No one would know. No one did. You set yourself the task of surviving, and you did. You lost that spaced-out feeling, you no longer flinched at sudden movements, your skin no longer shrank back to itself. You even forgot that that was how it was. You stopped thinking about yourself. You were strong, stronger than most others; you stood in front of a class of children and felt them draw from your strength.

And then there was the lover. He'd stroke your shoulder and tell you: 'You're such a strong person.'

⬥

In this opened-out landscape, the road that you lived on, which you'd always remembered as steeply inclined, was an innocent minor slope. Here at the bottom, in place of the grimy terrace where the woman stood staring, a wire fence enclosed a yard of shipping containers in primary colours, their bases washed by silvery weeds. Opposite, where once a high stone wall enclosed the grounds of a ruined mansion, a small housing estate of rosy brick had been built, and, as you watched, a man in a bright blue jumper came out to his car, whistling into the glassy twenty-first-century day.

There was nothing here of your past.

You should have been glad, but you found yourself ambushed by loss.

When you drove up the road and there was the terrace you lived in still standing, you felt something close to relief.

The bricks were clean now, the doors and windows replaced with white plastic, but there at the side of the end house was the high wooden fence your father once built.

You got out of the car and leaned your hands on the now-grey boards. You peered through a hole where a knot had dropped away in the years in between. Bright white slammed your eye: a kitchen extension had been built across the yard, blocking the view of the garden beyond. Your vision adjusted. Through windows in the near and far sides, a square of garden was still visible, and framed in that bright-green square was a boy, hands in pockets and foot on a ball, his bristly hair an aura in the sun.

You felt displaced.

It was ridiculous, you thought, you should turn around now, put it all behind you again, get back on the motorway, get home. But then there you were instead, driving over the space where the factory once stood, and up towards the village with the castle.

There were no fields now; to the left an industrial estate patchworked the hill, and a council estate tumbled away on the right. At the top, at the start of the village, nothing had altered: there at the start were the four Jacobean houses, giving way to two rows of nineteenth-century cottages that curved off around the crest of the hill. Yet the way it was now was not the way it had been your mind: sunk in wintry late-afternoon gloom. Now, in the spring midday, the houses baked like yeasty loaves, mullioned windows fizzing light.

You parked a little way into the village. Now, as then, there was no one about. You set off walking, the way you did with your sister all those years before.

You'd walk, the two of you, to where the cottages ended at a common, and there you'd stop before setting back again. You'd stand, arm in arm, looking out across the green at a copse in the distance, etched on a reddening sky like a drawing in a fairy-story book. You would shiver. It would be dark soon: you'd have to get back, you'd be in trouble all over again if you didn't, to the door in the fence, the grind through the cinders, the flinch of the back door opening, the blue swipe as your father looked up from his paper. There was no escape into a fairytale.

Now, all these years later, when you got to the end of the cottages you came up short. On the left, where you'd ex-pected the green to open out, was a high wall of privet, the roofs of established houses just visible beyond.

You were uneasy, troubled. You'd spent your life putting it all behind you, but now it felt important, imperative even, to have remembered this correctly, yet it seemed you hadn't.

Now you were somehow desperate to find the common. It must be further off the main road than you'd remembered. You turned into a side road between more high hedges. The wind dropped; the hidden gardens pooled with birdsong and the private hush of suburbia. You turned a corner: this would it be it, you felt sure. Blocking the way was a red-brick primary school, and beyond, a thick wood of sycamores, their tops swaying in the high-up wind. This couldn't be it at all. Your sense of loss increased.

As you reached the main road again you spotted the sign you missed when you turned in: *The Common*. You understood now: the green had been built on long ago, not long, probably, after you left the town, the copse, black and still and distant and enchanted in your memory, become those tossing schoolyard trees.

You felt relieved again, vindicated; yet also once again negated by the change. And seized by a sense of something important almost grasped but out of reach, something that needed to be retrieved.

There was a time once before when you had the urge to resurrect the memory. You wanted to tell the lover, you thought of it, had the urge. But you didn't, you thought better. You didn't want to make it a truth about you for him, since by then it wasn't the truth about you at all. But when, as he reached for his cigarettes, you noticed his scar, caught sight of the knife-kiss of silver on his inside wrist, and he saw you seeing, well then he told you – desperate, grateful to tell you – all the things he had suffered. He wanted you to know that that *was* the real truth about him.

He sat frozen, his face a mask as he remembered. You felt disturbed. The light in the room angled downwards and the shadows purpled.

But you thought: you were lucky, luckier than him. You'd

put your past pain behind you in a way that he hadn't, and it had made you strong.

⊖

Now, once more on the main road of the village, it came to you with a thud that you hadn't seen the castle.

How could that be? The way you remembered, it was unmissable, lowering and huge on a stony outcrop above the road.

It must be further on . . . But no, you were sure that this was as far as you and your sister ever came . . .

In the buffeting wind, you felt dizzy.

You opened up the map you'd brought from the car and found the road, coloured yellow. Yes, there was the castle, marked in gothic lettering, further on, in fact right at the far end of the road. You must, after all, have walked further than the common all those years ago. It seemed urgent now, somehow, that the details of the memory be accurate, yet here was the whole of it in doubt.

The wind flung your hair, flapped the map. You set off for the far end of the village. The gusts knocked you, sometimes against you, sometimes pushing you on. You felt disconnected, with the ground, with the surroundings, 30s semis you didn't remember set back behind long front gardens. Two teenage lads overtook you on skateboards, gliding with ease through the village and the twentieth-first-century day.

You reached the end of the road. You remembered none of it.

The area here, though, was recently redeveloped, with a small roundabout and two new roads, one curving off left around the far side of the hill, the other leading right into a bijou housing estate. Ahead was a landscaped walkway to the council houses pouring off down the hill.

Could the changes have brought the road further away from the castle? Could it be hidden behind the new buildings?

But surely it was more imposing than that . . .

A patrol car stopped beside you. A friendly young cop wound down his window and asked if you were lost. You'd passed the castle, he told you. You insisted you hadn't, and he looked at the map and agreed you were right, it should be right here.

'What's that back there, then?' he asked, pointing the way you'd both come.

You peered at the map, which showed a ruined priory near the start of the road but set well back. 'That's a priory,' you told him.

Why were you looking for the castle? he asked, and you told him, that as children you and your sister walked up from the town.

He cracked a laugh of surprise. 'You walked up through the estate?! Even *I* wouldn't walk up there!' He was very young, he couldn't imagine a time when the council estate with all its problems wasn't there.

The two feisty girls of his imagination, unfazed by the neighbourhood louts, rose up to replace your cowering, shivering selves.

And you felt effaced.

✧

You'd felt that before.

When the lover reached for his cigarettes, he had a way of doing it, dropping his arm in a curve, that made you think of someone drowning. He would light up and breathe, and his eyes would bruise sideways out of the present into the past.

In the beginning it was all you wanted, to rescue him from his past.

But you started to resent the way he gave you no option, the way, whenever he said you were strong, his mouth would then close in a line, his upper lip coming down like a lid.

✧

'Good luck looking for the castle!' The policeman moved off.

The two skateboarding lads, coming back, stopped and kicked up their boards and asked if you were doing a survey, eager to help. You saw yourself as they saw you, the kind of woman who'd be doing a survey, detached casual observer in leather jacket and jeans, someone in control. The image floated, disconnected from you.

'Trip down memory lane,' you told them, feeling fraudulent.

✧

When you said you couldn't go on, the lover went still. You touched his arm, but he didn't move. He didn't speak. His face was expressionless, his mouth an unyielding line. You even thought he might hit you.

Later you wondered. A man like your father: how could you ever have got involved?

⸏

'Are you lost?'

A round face with wire specs popped up from behind a low garden wall, and a stout man who'd been weeding unseen got to his feet.

You laid the map on the wall, and you and he looked at it together.

He scratched his head. Like the policeman, he'd thought the priory was a castle, and, though it was clearly marked on the map, he didn't know of any other castle just here. It must, he said, be a pretty inconspicuous ruin.

Could it be that you *invented* the castle of your memory? Imagined, *dreamt* your own past?

The wind grabbed the map, you had to secure it with your hand.

The man stood thinking, hands on hips, stomach swelling in a grease-marked sweater. 'There's lots of ruins in this area, though,' he said. 'Lots of history.'

His glasses blinked. All around the bright day glittered.

'Tell you what,' he said, 'I've got a friend who's a local historian. If anyone can tell you, he can. Come on in and I'll get you his email.'

You opened your mouth. You wanted to say that it wasn't that kind of history you were interested in, but you didn't want to, either, you couldn't. You couldn't tell the truth, that you were looking for a memory. It wasn't a memory people could believe, it didn't seem right, it didn't seem seemly, and you weren't even sure any more if you believed it yourself.

You followed him down the path as he waved at his weedy garden explaining that now he'd been made redundant he had time to tackle it at last. He led you round to the back of the house and a green space surrounded by tall trees.

Here there were hens, running free.

And you thought of the hens your mother kept at the bottom of the garden in the town down below.

They were his wife's hens, the man was telling you.

They strolled, lifting their legs with their measured clockwork motion, making their sound like a spring uncoiling.

The man led you up the steps and through the back door to a narrow untidy kitchen. You waited while he scrabbled between unwashed dishes through sifts of paper.

Leaf shadows simmered up and down the walls, trembled on the clutter. There was something, some truth, still out of reach but bubbling upwards now . . .

Behind you, triumphant, the man had found his friend's email. He wrote it down then led you out, past the hens and back down the long front garden to the gate. He said, 'Let's check the map again.'

You just wanted to go, to be alone, but you played along, you let him help you open out the map and pin it on the wall.

He gave a cry. He was pointing to the yellow line you thought you'd been following. 'This isn't the road!'

It was the bus route, he told you, approaching the village from the other side of the hill, and ending where the village road began. You understood now: the castle, after all, was at the start of the village; you'd driven past it before you parked, where, close and high up, it would be out of view from inside the car.

The map billowed, as if shrugging something off.

⊖

There was another fence your father erected: a high wire one for the hen run. He stood on steps fixing the wire, whistling with a sound like a faraway wind.

You went out to the hen run to call him for his tea. He had stopped whistling. He was leaning on one of the posts. He didn't see you approach. He looked up and saw you, and wiped his expression. But you'd seen it already: a faraway, helpless expression. A look of longing and loss. A look like a bruise.

⊖

'Which road did you live on?' the man wanted to know, and when you told him he cried, 'So did I!'

He folded up the map and handed it back. 'Know where you are now?'

You nodded, thinking of what he must have been like as a boy: confident, pleasant, a little plump, perhaps. Perhaps, as you and your sister made your timid way down the hill, he was one of the children running past . . .

Something happened to your memory. It widened, warmed: hot sun slid down the red-brick tannery wall, spilled onto the terraces, turning them russet, and spread in a glow over the town, melting it into the present.

THE RELENTLESS PULL OF GRAVITY

A black hole is an object that is so compact its gravitational force is strong enough to prevent light, or anything else, escaping.

The woman knows, without seeing, that someone has died.

She stands on the neatly cut lawn and it comes to her first as the sense of a hole punched in the universe. She identifies the sounds then, floating over her high garden wall from the lock on the old canal: the tight commands of a tragedy managed, and now and then low exclamations of concern.

She stays still beneath the beech tree, on the lawn beside her glassy house, and absorbs the things she can't see: the white vehicles on the bridge, the luminous jackets and flurry of movement beneath the canopy of trees, the body pulled from the water.

And it comes back, her old feeling of teetering on the edge of a fathomless pit.

That evening in the pub the woman's son hears what happened. One of the winos, off his head on cider no doubt,

Note: All quotes in italics are taken or adapted from the Hubble 2011 website 'Gravity's Relentless Pull'

35

staggering along the towpath during the night and stumbling into the deep brick-sided lock.

The son and his friends and the landlord snort wryly at the comedy, then shake their heads in sympathy at the degradation and sadness of some lives.

The son walks home through the falling dusk and back into town, past the long low factory where once his father made engines and which, after his father's death, he sold off to the electronics firm.

Just before his mother's house the road goes over the canal, near the lock where the drowning occurred. Here, under the bridge, the winos often gather. They squat there on the cobbles, making way as you pass if you're walking your dog: lice-ridden bodies on one side and the deep dark water only an inch off on the other. They pull up their knees with an air which may be irony or may be not, and even now they fill him, a man of forty-five, with unease.

He turns in through the gates of his mother's glass-fronted house, the house where he spent his teenage years, and crunches up the drive to tell her what he knows about the drowning just beyond her garden wall.

'Oh, that's terrible!' she says. She stops, looking up at him, little as she is now, her hand above the kettle, knuckles swollen with age.

He remembers his mother's hand without those swellings, held high above his head. He remembers her face smooth, her jawline firm, her eyebrows dark commas. After all these years he still sees it, that image, he has to look through it to her present incarnation, and it irritates him that he does. It squeezes his stomach, this sense of things being *stuck*.

Near a black hole distortions in space and time become so strong that time behaves in unexpected ways.

He is irritated too, as usual, by her reaction, the way such things always upset her. 'That's terrible!' she keeps saying, shaking her head as she pours his tea and then sits across from him while he drinks. He says – he can't help it, though he knows it will make her even more unhappy: 'Well, it's not as if he had much chance of any decent fate.' Dismissive of the wino, and also of her: he's made it clear she's alone with her feelings. And then he feels bad: after only two years she's still grieving his father, and any death is bound to bring it all back. And the fact is, he could do without upsetting her further, what with everything else: the slump in the property market, the impending divorce, his teenage daughters slipping out of his influence and running wild. He knows his mother will be thinking him callous. In spite of all her efforts, she'll be thinking, she turned a callous brute out into the world. Maybe that's what he is. And this is what irritates him most of all about her: that always, whenever they talk, he ends up with a jaundiced view of himself.

He stands, he checks the locks, checks that she's safe in the glassy castle, and crunches in the dark down the drive.

All matter in a black hole is squeezed into a region of infinitely small volume called the central singularity. The event horizon is an imaginary sphere that [marks] the closest you can get to the central singularity [without being pulled into it].

The woman's bedroom faces over the lawn towards the canal. She thinks about the fact that she was lying beneath the window as, metres off in the dark, the man swayed on the edge of the lock. She was turning beneath the duvet, perhaps, as he floundered, opened his mouth to cry and it filled with icy fluid. She lifts her hand to draw the bedroom curtain. Here, at night, away from the street lights, nothing out there can be seen. The thought obsesses her: her one side and him the other, divided yet joined by that dark vibrating space. The image surrounds her.

She begins to undress.

She doesn't feel old, the woman, although her son treats her as such. She can't deny the number of years that have passed, but here she is taking off her cardi with just the same gesture, reflected in the very same mirror, the one with which they furnished the room when they first moved in with their eleven-year-old son, a couple in the flush of successful early middle age. Where did they go, those years? How did they go? Fast, so fast it didn't seem like time passing. She feels like Alice: she was dropped from a bright day where her husband stood young and tall and dark-suited beside her, to that hospital room where he lay dying of an old man's disease, shrivelled and strapped to machines which in the end they turned off.

The woman's son drives his younger daughter to Mac-Donald's. She is silent, skewed away from him. She is chewing gum. She is fourteen. He hates it, the exaggerated yet slovenly way she chews, the shortness of her skirt; he aches for the way she'll be judged for it, he thinks, and he hates that he's now helpless to do anything about that, to affect the way she'll be treated in this world. Indeed, he has the feeling that anything he says will now automatically provoke opposition and rebellion. When his wife decided to divorce him, his daughters did, too, it seems. It's worse: the way she chews strikes him as insolent provocation directed specifically at him. So yes, he also hates those things about her for himself. And once again he feels trapped into a selfish impulse he'd rather not own, for which he can be justifiably hated, and indeed hates himself.

He says, 'Did you hear about the man who was drowned in the canal just by Grandma's house?'

She moves a fraction back in his direction – his chest twitches – her eyes widening with an interest she can't hide. 'No.'

He tells her what he knows: a homeless man, one of those who hang around beneath the bridge, drunk of course.

She doesn't answer, but glancing sideways he sees her scanning and processing the information. Accepting it. Accepting something from him.

He's encouraged. Just a moment ago she turned over the book in her lap (she'll read the whole time in MacDonald's, he knows), and he saw the title: *Our Universe: Luck or Design?* He says: 'Did you know that the universe is quite literally filled with black holes?'

The slam of her hostility: 'So?'

Time passes, he thinks, things change. Young people take for granted the existence of black holes. It was news to him, at fifteen. And he's back in the moment, a night when he and his father have set up the new telescope, away from the beech tree on the lawn. 'Too much bloody light pollution,' his father is saying – even then, thirty years back, it was a problem – his lean body bent away over the instrument. And he, the boy, was made for once only briefly tense by the irritation in his father's voice. He was dancing, impatient, desperate to see, gazing up at the pinpoints that could still be seen through the sulphur, waiting to find them transformed, and imagining all the other, possible worlds. 'Come on, Dad, let me see!'

His dad straightened up, and the boy could see in the filtered light that his cheek was rippling: he was grinding his teeth, a bad sign, and all the joy of the stargazing enterprise drained away for the boy. And that was when his father told him: the most important bodies in the universe are the ones he wouldn't be able to see, the ones which for a century and a half they'd called invisible stars, but had recently defined as black holes.

Black holes grow in mass by capturing nearby material, [though] a black hole can only capture objects that come very close to it.

When the woman was twenty-one she saw the time ahead as a dance floor, like the one across which her husband, a grinning stranger, came swaggering towards her. He was new to the town, a fellow with a Scottish accent, in a Teddyboy jacket and with his hair in a greasy DA, a lad really, in spite of his thirty years and her father's horror that she should give herself to so much older a man.

He made a beeline and stood in front of her, looking her up and down, not bothering to hide his appreciation: her white shoes, her back-combed hair, her yellow dress with its full net petticoat. All boldness he was, all good-natured cheek, and so she laughed and gave him her hand, and he swirled her out onto the dance floor, a yellow star, a bright sun.

That was how he seemed to come to her; out of the future, sweeping her up into it, a future of excitement promised by his grin.

Oh yes, he was dynamic; oh yes, he could charm the rest of the world, the bosses in the tools factory where he worked; later on, their takeover rivals; years after, the bank manager, making his successful bid to own it all. He ended up the well-off businessman her father would have wanted, the life and soul of the parties in the big glass house he built.

A black hole is born when a [massive star] becomes unable to withstand the force of its own gravity.

The trouble was, she faltered, right there near the beginning. Something about him troubled her, though she couldn't place it. She took the ring off, eclipsed the diamond, handed it back. She'd been too hasty: what she needed was time to know her own feelings. She thought that, thirty years old, nearly ten years older, he'd understand.

When she stepped into the pitch-black ginnel between the pavement and the door of his flat, she knew what had happened. There are things you can know without seeing; there are things you can know before they happen. Time isn't linear: she was always afterwards sure of that. His door wasn't locked; she let herself in. He was slumped on the sofa, an empty pill bottle on the floor.

She knew then that she need not have faltered after all: her spirit flew to bring him back to her, across the light years he'd already travelled, his heart pumped by the ambulance crew, blue lights spinning him back in defiance of all the natural laws.

There was something he hadn't told her, she now discovered. That once, in his native Scotland, he'd slept under bridges curled around despair, the cries of seagulls scooping his skull. Despair, it turned out, was the flipside of his grinning charm.

She had flown to him, and he rallied. And in defiance of all the natural laws of that small town, he kept intact his cheerful public persona (an accident, he'd said it was, that rush in the ambulance, laughing about it later with his mates in the pub.)

Yet all their married life she could feel that darkness pulling. There'd be the moment when they shut the door on their charmed departed guests, and his grin would fade and his cheek begin working, and she'd feel the nearness of a vacuum that could suck them all in, him and her and their growing son. The trouble was, she'd failed him once and he could never believe she wouldn't fail him again. She worked so hard to prove him wrong and keep the three of them faced towards happiness. And on the surface she succeeded: he never again made such an attempt, and they kept the truth of his past from their son. It was a force, though, that she couldn't completely control: nothing could prevent his private dark moods, or her own fearfulness, and nothing could prevent the effect of those on their son.

Black holes completely erase all of the other complex properties of the objects that they swallow.

The man's daughter gets out of the car outside the gate. She did read the book the whole time she ate her burger. The more he tried to talk to her in that voice, over-jolly, the more she thought For god's sake! (all those years that he was so bad-tempered and morose!), the more she just wanted to curl away from him.

He leans over the seat to look out at her. 'Next Saturday, maybe?'

She can hardly bring herself to answer, because what's the point of these meetings, of him trying to pull it all together, when he was the one who sent things spinning apart with his stupid depression, so long ago? She shrugs and says, 'Whatever,' avoiding his eyes. As she says it, it comes to her: the thing that she can't stand in his voice and his eyes is pleading.

The car pulls off and leaves a space which feels like a vacuum.

She thinks again, For god's sake! because in her throat there's a lump, which is stupid, really stupid, she is not a girl who cries at all.

Current theories predict that all the matter in a black hole is piled up in a single point at the centre. We do not understand how this singularity works.

That evening, in the place where the canal runs through the centre of the town, the down-and-outs and alcoholics gather. To passers-by they're a strange-looking group, coalescing and bobbing apart as new bodies arrive, in mushroom hats pulled onto Brillo-pad hair, coats with drunken hems, old leggings pulled down over near-splitting trainers. They carry bundles: the usual clinking plastic carriers, and, some of them, objects in battered cases over shoulders or tucked under arms. At last they're all there, and straggling but purposeful, they set off along the canal towards the lock.

To understand a black hole requires a theory unifying both the theory of gravity and the theory of quantum mechanics, but how it would work is still unknown.

The man's daughter is not sure what brings her that evening to the bridge over the canal; really, with all the trouble, Mum and Dad not speaking to each other, she's been avoiding this part of town. She's leaning over and staring at the lock when the band of winos appears, coming into view from under the awning of leaves. They stop at the lock. The first man puts down his bundle and stands with his hands on his hips as the others gather round. In near silence, they line up the bottles on the stones. The ones with the cases open them up and take out a violin, a concertina and a flute. Someone speaks, a joke she can't quite hear about not going too near the edge. The air cracks open with guffaws.

She raises her eyes to the high brick wall behind them, where her grandmother lives. Maybe she'll call, she hasn't seen her gran in a while, even if there's a risk her dad'll be there.

And she thinks, For god's sake! because she finds herself weeping.

The central singularity might form a bridge to another universe.

The woman is in the garden behind the wall when the wake begins.

She has heard the laughter, the men's bellows and the women's cackles, and now the concertina bounces into it all. The drink-cracked voices jump to join it.

The violin starts up, adding a descant, a sound like the cry of a seagull, soaring into the evening sky.

We know now that black holes evaporate, slowly returning their energy to the universe.

CLARRIE AND YOU

Often when you think of Clarrie, you see her in her bright-green swimsuit, fifteen years old, an Amazon mermaid picking her way across the rocks towards the sea, hands flapping like flippers already, the sea and sky behind her a freshly-painted backdrop. She would get to the place where the rocks fell away in a cliff-face just beneath the water, a place where you, the smaller younger sister, would never dare go because you couldn't swim, and she dived. Then there she was, way out, her white cap bobbing, as if she'd forgotten the world on the shore.

You were jealous, of course.

Or you think of her earlier, leaping the glassy puddles in the lane to your gran's where you'd often be sent for the day. She seemed to fly; she'd take off on her muscular legs – sure-footed, never landing in cowpats – then run, leaving you to pick your way around the pools, afraid of the ghost dog someone had seen by the stile and desperately hoping she'd stop to watch a bird. She knew the names of all the birds, Clarrie, the little dull ones that most people don't even know are different from each other. She knew all the flowers, she could identify every variety of tree.

Not that many people would know: in school she never opened her mouth. She was big and she was strong, but she was cripplingly shy. In company she'd hang back, saying nothing. People thought she was stupid, when really she just wasn't very worldly-wise.

'Look after Clarrie,' your mother would tell you quietly before the two of you went out together – you on your spindly legs and not even coming up to Clarrie's shoulder, and Clarrie most likely to shoot off without you the moment you were out of sight.

There are things you don't want to remember, because doing so makes you guilty, after all these years and at your time of life, of ridiculous sibling rivalry. The way that sometimes, when Clarrie's friend Minnie went with you to Granny's and however hard you begged they wouldn't let you play, Granny would take Clarrie's side.

You'd dance around her pleading: 'Please, Clarrie, *please!*' but she wouldn't answer, she turned away, her shoulders set, stubborn and resentful, and in the end Granny would tell you off: 'Leave Clarrie alone.'

Clarrie was Granny's favourite. 'She's one of us,' Granny would say, by which she meant big like Granny herself and everyone else on your father's side. And of course, at ten years old, you were jealous of *that*.

You'd insist, full of injustice and a sense of exile: 'But I want to play!'

'It's not always what *you* want,' Granny would tell you. 'Don't be so selfish.'

And Clarrie would sit silent, and Minnie, censorious and righteous, glared at you out of a mass of curly hair.

Of course, what you didn't guess then was that Clarrie was jealous of *you*, of the way you could talk to anyone, ten to the dozen, and the fact that people saw you as the clever one.

Later, Granny would tell your mother, and you – meant to look after Clarrie, not go picking quarrels – were in trouble all over again. And once more Clarrie said nothing, simply sat there looking at the floor, as your family reputation was being laid down: the selfish pesky one.

That was all before the war.

You think of Clarrie, too, in wartime: eighteen years old, statuesque and big-busted in her WAAF uniform, square shoulders held back the way she'd been trained, but still with a diffident set to her frame, and a tendency to giggle.

There's a scene that often comes back to you, although, for more than one reason, you wish that it didn't.

You were outside the Mess up at the camp: you, Clarrie and Clarrie's new boyfriend Robert whom later she'd marry, a tall airman with glasses and prominent teeth and large ears.

You were nervous. He was a strait-laced chap, Robert, and you sensed he didn't like you. You knew in your heart by this time that Clarrie was jealous, of your small slim figure, your sense of fashion, the easy way you had of making friends, your academic success. You knew she felt it unfair, and of course Robert would know how she felt.

And something else was making you on edge: your own fiancé Jimmy. You were all going to the pictures, the four of you together, but you were being delayed because Jimmy was still in the Mess.

So handsome he was, Jimmy: hooded eyes and sharp jawline, and that wicked crooked grin, and everyone loved him for his charm. He was making you late, though, and Robert was obviously annoyed.

Clarrie gave her awkward little giggle, and you did what you always did when you were nervous, you gabbled. On and on you gabbled, you could hear yourself doing it. And then you saw it: Robert and Clarrie exchanging the look that told you what you'd done: cemented your reputation as the one who would never shut up or leave anyone alone.

✧

'Olive?'

Always at the sound of her voice it's those images that first come to you.

She was ringing to tell you the details of Robert's funeral.

Her voice, as always, was plaintive – all those years of being bossed around by Robert – and today it was weak with grief.

You knew what she'd been going through, you'd gone through it yourself with Jimmy ten years before: trailing to the hospital every day, Robert so far gone that in the end he didn't know her, Clarrie hoping against hope, but knowing really she was watching him die.

This was Thursday, and the funeral, she said, would be Tuesday.

'Eleven o'clock.'

You were surprised it was so early. You repeated it: 'Eleven o'clock?' It was such a long way, down there in the South-West, and you up here in the Midlands. You'd have to go the previous day.

She said awkwardly: 'I'm afraid we wouldn't be able to put you up.'

You were a little hurt, and then quickly ashamed. Of course, Clarrie would have a houseful already – her three children and maybe their spouses, and even perhaps the grandchildren.

You said hastily, 'Oh, of course not!'

But you didn't much fancy staying in a hotel. You said, 'No problem, Clarrie, I'll come and get back in one day. I'll get a very early train.'

She didn't answer straight away. You were standing at the window and the silence went on so long you watched a wren pop out of the ivy on the wall outside and hop several steps up the greenery before popping back in again.

Then Clarrie said: 'Well, I'll give you instructions for getting to the crematorium.'

You were taken aback. Surely she'd want you to travel with her to the crematorium, the way she and Robert did with you when Jimmy died?

She was saying she had to go, and before you knew it she'd got off the phone.

You considered. Of course: the funeral was so early she reckoned you wouldn't have time to get to the house beforehand. Obviously, when you thought about it, you wouldn't. You chided yourself for letting those old childhood feelings of exclusion dog you into old age.

Elsie, too, your brother's widow, lived a distance from Clarrie, if not as far as you.

When Elsie rang you later that day, you said, 'I'm

surprised they made it so early when we've got to travel.'

You thought of Elsie as you first knew her, a skinny watchful girl who'd moved to the village from the town. A puny town-girl you and Clarrie thought her, but then later your brother married her and she put you to shame, trudging in her wellies to help with the lambing, wading up to her neck with the trawlnet in the rock pools, gutting the fish in the back of the van.

And later, because Clarrie and Robert lived nearer than you and Jimmy, and so were able to visit more often, she and your brother and Clarrie and Robert became good friends.

Elsie said with surprise: 'Well, they couldn't have held it *much* later. It's at four in the afternoon.'

You told her, 'No, it's at eleven!'

How could Elsie have got it so wrong?

She said in bewilderment: 'I'll ring Clarrie back and check.'

Half an hour later she rang you again.

'Yes, Olive, the funeral's definitely at four.'

Was it you who had got it wrong?

She sounded strangely embarrassed.

But, no, you remembered, you'd repeated it to Clarrie: *Eleven o' clock?*, with emphasis, precisely because you were so surprised, and she didn't contradict you.

'What did Clarrie say,' you asked Elsie, 'when you said I thought it was at eleven?'

There was a brief silence, and then Elsie said in a tight voice: 'I didn't mention it.'

This was even odder. You felt confused. Surely she'd have

mentioned it, it was her reason for ringing Clarrie back and checking . . .

It hit you: Clarrie had lied to you about the time, and Elsie knew it.

Elsie said, with an air of quickly changing the subject, 'I'd rather get back the same night, but they're trying to persuade me to stay. They say they've got room.'

You reeled it back in your head, the conversation with Clarrie, and you heard it all now: the hesitancy, which you'd taken as the hesitancy of grief, with which she'd told you the time. The embarrassment: embarrassment at lying. And when she said she couldn't put you up, the stubborn note of old.

Then the silence when you said you'd come anyway: the silence of shock, and the old resentment at your persistence.

And if you were intent on coming anyway, she would give you instructions for getting to the crematorium. In other words, she wouldn't have you at the house.

But why?

'Why on earth would she do that?' your children cried. 'She isn't like that, Clarrie!'

Well, no, she wasn't. Were you wrong? Had you only imagined that Clarrie had said eleven o'clock? Had you imagined that you'd repeated it? Were you going senile? You could see that the thought had entered your middle-aged children's heads . . .

No, she wasn't like that, Clarrie, passive Clarrie who'd never say boo to a goose, who'd spent her life being bossed by others, who couldn't even make a phone call to you, her sister, without her husband Robert butting in on the extension.

And then it came to you. The quality of sound whenever Robert did that, picked up and listened in: slightly hollow, with a faint high background buzz. That sound was there again during the recent conversation.

Someone else had been listening in.

Someone else had heard you repeat, *Eleven o'clock?* and failed to contradict, failed to own up even to being there. Someone who didn't want you at the funeral.

Clarries' eldest daughter Janet.

So often when you think of Janet, you see a chubby five-year-old in shorts with her hair in bunches, fishing in the shallow rock pools, those days after the war when you and Clarrie were still living in the village, when Robert was in Malaysia, and Clarrie, still wearing her green swimsuit, still giggly, was missing him and sad.

But also you think of Janet as a rangy young woman, handsome with Robert's strong features, standing here in your kitchen in the Midlands, one bright summer evening during the eighties, when she and her husband had been on business in Scotland and were calling in for tea on their way back down south. Just before they got here something had gone badly wrong with their car, but the local garage was shut for the evening, so though nothing was said, it was taken for granted they'd be staying the night.

You and she were washing up when she asked you, pointed and careful: 'Aunty Olive, why do you go to Granma's every single month to clean her house?'

You froze.

Yes, you *were* doing that. Your widowed mother was failing. She had a bad heart; for the past eighteen months her eyesight had been going, and now she was finding it difficult to walk. But then, Janet was implying, why did *you* need to go and clean for her, when you lived so far off and had a business to run, and when your brother's wife Elsie, a full-time housewife living right across the road, was looking after her already?

Janet stood with a bunch of gleaming teaspoons, waiting for an answer.

And the answer, the reason, bubbled in your chest and pressed against your throat, and stuck.

A year before you had gone on one of your six-monthly visits back home.

You opened the door of your mother's cottage and found her sitting beside a dead congealed fire. Every surface was covered in dust, the carpet was unswept, dirty dishes were piled in the sink. She had a condition, conjunctivitis, for which she was meant to be being treated, but her eyes were red and weeping, and her prescription, two weeks old, lay on the sideboard, her medicine uncollected.

You tidied up and made her as comfortable as you could, then marched across the road to Elsie's.

A ghost answered the door. Her face was white; she was thinner than ever.

It was all too much for her, she told you, the shopping and cooking and cleaning for your mother, it was making her ill. She spoke in a hollow whisper: she'd lost her voice.

'*You'll* have to do it,' she told you. 'You'll just have to come down more often.'

You could hardly abandon your business, but you did agree to go for a few days every month, to take over the care of your mother and catch up on the cleaning and get in supplies.

Elsie added, 'She's *your* mother, after all,' which, after all, was fair enough.

But then she was Clarrie's mother too – Clarrie who didn't work, and lived so much nearer and came often to stay with Elsie and your brother for days of walking and fishing. It was very quickly clear that Elsie had shared the problem with no one else, not even Clarrie.

Your heart sinking, you guessed why. In that place at that time, a rural village in the eighties, people would be all too ready to criticise a woman for abandoning her traditional role. And Robert, strait-laced Robert, could be more censorious than anyone. She was afraid of what he'd think of her. After all, she would know what he thought of you.

Clearly, she hadn't told your mother. 'Elsie will do that!' your mother told you irritably as you washed the windows and laundered her sheets. She didn't understand why your visits had all of a sudden become so frequent, and why you spent them doing housework. You knew she thought you a busybody, and probably that as usual you were jealous, jealous of her closeness with Elsie, and you couldn't deny – hating yourself for conforming to the family expectations – that under the circumstances, you *were* a little jealous, and not a little hurt.

You couldn't tell her the truth about Elsie, you didn't

feel you could betray her, and anyway, with your reputation, you'd look petty and vengeful. It didn't matter, you decided, as long as your mother was cared for. You wouldn't let it upset you: you, a woman running a business, with a life of her own elsewhere. You were bigger than that.

One day you went to collect your mother's pension and there in the post office was Clarries' old friend, Minnie. The girl with a mass of curls was now a stout matron with cropped hair, but as she made her way purposefully across towards you, the same old accusing look was her eyes. 'Olive,' she demanded, 'why do you keep coming down and making such a fuss of looking after your mother? You know there's no need. It's not fair on Elsie: it makes it look as if she's not bothering.'

You opened your mouth, but your unspoken pact with Elsie stopped any words.

She said, 'Well, Olive, we all know what you're like,' and turned away and walked out.

And now here it was happening with Janet your niece all over again, and once more, the truth, Elsie's secret, jammed in your throat.

Janet gave a nod. She placed the spoons on the table and, avoiding your eye, said with a knowing censorious smile: 'Well, we all know why you do it, Aunty Olive.'

What on earth could she be implying?

You knew they'd always seen you as selfish, but surely they couldn't think that you, a woman who owned a business, were after whatever your mother – whose house was rented, whose savings were probably non-existent – would leave when she died?

You were so upset you couldn't speak. You walked out of the kitchen and pretended to be busy in the utility room.

You thought of them all discussing you: Robert going on about you, the whole thing leaking out to be the talk of the village, Elsie keeping quiet, shamefully maybe, but secure in the protection of your reputation.

Just then the men came in from a stroll in the garden and your mouth jerked open, and before you could help it these words burst through the block in your throat: 'Well, Janet and Derek will have to get going: they'll need to drive slowly in that car.'

All three of them stared at you, disbelieving: surely Janet and Derek couldn't drive in that car, surely they were staying?

But then Jimmy gave you his Look.

Quizzical, shrewd it was, that look of Jimmy's. Very brief, sussing things out in a second or two, and then gone. The look of the conman, of course, a man who dealt in silk stockings during the war. But also the look of a man who *understands*, who knows exactly the score without a word being spoken. He didn't question you, or argue, he simply agreed.

And Janet and her husband had to leave, drive two hundred miles in a car that could conk out at any time, though thankfully it didn't.

You worried about them all evening, and were hugely relieved to hear next day that they'd got back safely after all. You worried they'd all be offended and furious, and expected a harangue from Robert. But neither he nor Clarrie mentioned what had happened, and you thought then that maybe Janet and Derek hadn't found it such a big deal, and you needn't have worried after all. You even thought that perhaps your notion of what they thought of you had all along been paranoid.

Now, at Robert's death, you understood it had been a huge deal. Why should they put Olive up, Janet would be thinking as she organised the funeral, when she did that to me? Why, come to that, should Olive even *be* at Dad's funeral, when he so disliked her? And Clarrie, so easily bullied, would be told what to say, while Janet listened in . . .

You ran it again in your mind, the conversation with Clarrie, and what you heard now was how miserable she sounded about it all.

So you didn't go to Robert's funeral. You sent flowers. They'd said they didn't want them, but you sent them specifically for Clarrie, to arrive when it was over, to express your solidarity as well as your condolence, to acknowledge that the problem was not between you and her.

And that day you tried to keep busy and think of other things. You washed some jumpers, and as you stood at the sink you kept seeing the wren take insects in its beak into the ivy where it must be nesting. Funny, the way it moved along in a straight smooth line, as if it didn't have legs, as if it were a mechanical thing on wheels, then flicked up and flew straight in, and the place where it had gone into the ivy was covered completely, so you'd never guess there was an entrance there.

In the evening Clarrie rang you to thank you for the flowers. She seemed more relaxed, and you felt relieved.

She told you in detail about the funeral, the number of cars they'd had to hire, the hotel they'd had to book to accommodate all of Richard's old colleagues, and the food they'd had for the reception. On and on she went, and that old feeling crept up on you: you began to have the sense that she was talking to herself, not you. She made no mention of your absence. There was, you began to realise, no hint of regret that you hadn't been there. By not going, you thought, you had let her off the hook and she was simply relieved.

You felt stung.

Elsie hadn't stayed over after all, and Clarrie said suddenly, as if it were a matter of great importance: 'I've rung Elsie, and she got home safely.'

At that – that discrimination – you couldn't help it, a bubble erupted from your throat: 'Clarrie, *why* wasn't I welcome at the funeral?'

It floated off and it couldn't be retrieved. There was a terrible silence, and you could picture her, shocked, confused, routed, shamed.

She said faintly, 'Of course you'd have been welcome!'

You could sense her horror, and were aghast yourself, but you were bursting with injustice, the way they'd always damned you as a gabbling pest while ensuring your silence and compliance. You were furious with Clarrie for always going along with it all, and with yourself for a lifetime of going along with it too.

You said, 'But Clarrie, you told me the funeral was at eleven when it was at four!'

She said, 'I didn't!' but it came out in a gasp.

You couldn't stop yourself. 'Well, you didn't invite me to

the house. You said you'd tell me how to go straight to the crematorium.'

'I didn't!' She was starting to cry.

Then voices started up in the background. 'Mum, come away from the phone!' 'Don't talk to her!'

She said, her voice mushy with tears, 'Olive, I can't talk to you when you're like this,' and she put the phone down.

You stood there, still holding the receiver, a woman who was so self-centred she'd pick a quarrel with her sister on the day of her sister's husband's funeral.

And her children told her not to have anything to do with you again.

⊸

You know they did because she told you. She defied them.

That's the thing about Clarrie: she's often easily bullied, but she can also be stubborn.

She said, 'I want to sort out what happened between us.' Her voice was still plaintive, but there was an edge of determination. You had an image of her striding back out of the sea in her green swimsuit, water streaming from her strong limbs.

You said, 'Clarrie, it's best if we forget it.'

She sounded surprised. She said, upset and worried, 'But Olive, we're sisters, we can't have things unspoken between us.'

Funny, Clarrie being the one to plead, and you the one to insist on silence.

But after all, when it came to it, you couldn't have it all

untangled it all with words, you couldn't have things dragged up. To explain why you sent Janet packing that evening would be to expose Elsie's deceit. And in order to stop Clarrie thinking you were being petty, you wouldn't resist explaining how they'd always all got you wrong, and – because it's still so painful – you'd go and mention that evening long ago outside the Mess, when Robert stared at you gabbling and made up his mind you were a bothersome pest. You'd have to say the real reason you were gabbling and panicking, and give away Jimmy's secret, which, like Elsie's, you've kept to this day.

So handsome he was, Jimmy, so charming, so popular with all the other airmen; everyone was drawn to him.

Looking back, in some deep part of you you'd half-guessed what he was up to as you waited, not just some black-market deal. You suppose if you hadn't you wouldn't have seen what you did that evening.

You were watching the Mess doorway over Robert's shoulder.

Someone came out, not Jimmy. He stopped to light a fag and stood there inhaling.

And then Jimmy did come out and you saw it, the look that passed between them: brief, gone in an instant, but a look of understanding, the score agreed without a word spoken. And then the other man looked away, and Jimmy passed him by and they were electric, you could see, with the effort of not acknowledging each other.

You'd half-guessed, but you didn't want to know.

For the whole of your marriage you didn't want to know.

Some things there's just no point dwelling on.

'Leave it, Clarrie,' you told her on the phone, and she did.

You put down the phone and listened to the wren's bubbling eruptions of sound. Such a very little bird, and such a huge song.

A MATTER OF LIGHT

1816

May 1st

Having never been a man much given to journal-making but spending my life in the practical matters of trade, I am minded now, in my seventy-sixth year and possessing greater leisure (my youngest son having taken on the greater burden of our business), to write of certain curious phenomena of light which I have recently witnessed within the walls of my home. To my knowledge no other member of my household has likewise made such sightings, for which I must be grateful, since there is a strangeness about them that could unsettle those of weak or uneducated mind.

All of my acquaintance, here and abroad, will vouch for me as a rational man, and I mean to set down in the spirit of scientific observation the particulars of these incidents, which have indeed occurred in broad daylight, and in a house but twenty-five years built, to my own commission and personal specification, and thus no likely repository for hauntings by previous deceased incumbents, even should one hold with the desire or ability of unquiet spirits to wander into our physical domain.

My house, standing as it does on an open hill just beyond the sweep of the town, faces not to the past but to the future, with clean lines and spacious rooms looking out to the rear down a hill towards the river and the misty hills beyond, and equipped with the latest devices for household convenience. My study is a room of calm proportions and, being on the ground floor, lit by one of the tallest windows, a place conducive to clarity of thought, contemplative study and the judicious conduct of business transactions. It is in this room that two days ago the first of the events to which I refer occurred.

It was mid-morning. I was alone and at my desk, reading an account by the Reverend Smythe of an attempt to transfer mulberry trees to warmer climes. The sun made a wide beam across the beige carpet in the centre of the room. I stood from my desk beside the window and crossed to the bookcase on the left-hand wall. As I did so, a movement to the right caught my eye. I thought that my servant had entered unnoticed, but in the next moment I knew I remained quite alone. I considered that my movement across the room had created an answering shadow, until I saw that my shade was falling away from me in the opposite direction, across the beige carpet and onto the wall on the left.

In truth, it was at the time a little thing, for my mind was much on the mulberry tree and its transplantation, and my curiosity was mild as I stepped back to the window and looked out to see what reflection or refraction had thrown perhaps the shadow of a bird against the usual trajectory. Looking out I saw nothing but the empty road and the rise beyond nodding with cowslips, and my thoughts returned to my studies.

I should have thought no more of it, had not something further occurred yesterday afternoon.

It is true that, since my wife is a fastidious keeper of this house, in spite of our large windows we are often much shrouded in shadow, the curtains pulled to protect the furnishings from bleaching by the sun. The lower staircase, however, is ever an airy sweep of light, its pale stone and open ironwork balustrade lit by a long window that looks out to the westerly hills. Yesterday afternoon I was mounting the first flight when I noticed on the wall beside the window the shadow of a man, head and shoulders sans periwig, merging below into a less distinct column. I looked around me quickly, expecting to see someone behind down the stairs or up on the landing. No one was there, but it struck me that it should have been strange even had they been so, for light comes only from the uncurtained window, thus casting shadows in the opposite direction, and no mirror is hung on any of the walls or on the landing above or in the hall down below to send back any rays. When I looked back the shadow had gone, and I will confess that I did then suffer a moment's unease, and the sense of encountering a Being, and the hairs on my neck did prick, before I mastered such thoughts that belong to base and irrational lore.

It is a most curious phenomenon which I cannot account for by my own previous studies of refraction, and which has much excited my scientific curiosity. I have this day sent to London for a copy of Thomas Young's paper to the Royal Society concerning the properties of light.

May 6th

I have perused Mr Young's experiments which proved that light is capable of being bent (and is thus made of waves rather than corpuscles as had been previously held), including his double-slit experiment in which two beams of light interfering with each other did indeed create stripes of shadow. But this yet does not explain how any shadow so created should appear on my wall quite against any beams of light entering my stairway.

I shall watch for further instances and record them carefully. I have all my life endeavoured to avoid the sin of pride, disliking ostentation in matters of both material wealth (I have ensured that my home, though large, is simply furnished) and intellect, yet I cannot but feel that to make a discovery that may contribute to the greater field of scientific knowledge would be the crowning glory of an assiduous and careful life.

I have not shared with my wife this hope, nor anything of the circumstance. She is stout of heart but she has suffered with her health since we settled in this rheumy part of the world; moreover, she has never put behind her the old superstitions, and would conclude that we have been invaded by ghosts.

May 8th

I have once more witnessed the shadow on the stairs. All was as before apart from the time of day and the fact that on this occasion I watched the shape disappear, which occurred not instantly, as with a sudden change of light or movement away of an object, but gradually, the object fading slowly before my eyes until no smudge of it remained. This pleases me, confirming perhaps some new character of light as yet un-observed and requiring investigation, light bending perhaps without the aid of mirrors from another vicinity altogether, and explaining those distortions which throughout history have been taken to be ghosts.

May 10th

No further occurrence of the light/shadow phenomenon, but I have been much taken up with other matters, not only my ship coming to harbour and involving me and my son with merchants, but another mystery in my household, one involv-ing sound.

I was in the drawing room alone, waiting for my wife to join me, when I heard someone whisper, it seemed from over near the door. I peered but was blinded by the beam of sun coming through the half-drawn curtains, and could make out nothing in the gloom beyond. The whisper came again, a rustle that resolved itself into what seemed to me a human voice, though I could not make out the words. 'Who is there?' I asked, stepping into the gloom. My eyes accustomed them-selves, and I saw that there was no one there. My sight lighted on the horn of the speaking tube, my house being most use-fully equipped with an ingenious system, still unknown to many. A series of tubes connects the kitchen to the upper rooms, the servants being summoned by blowing through a horn at the upper end and activating a whistle at the lower, so saving much running about of servants, and the purse of the master who may thus employ fewer. I deduced that this was whence the sound had come, the whistle at the lower end having become detached and sound from the kitchen allowed to travel upwards. I tried it, my wife just then entering the room. The whistle sounded at the other end, and we thought that it must have been quickly replaced, yet when the maid appeared and my wife called her to account she averred that the whistle had been in place all along, and her manner was so sincerely upset that I do not know if the problem is a mechanical one needing my attention or a servant problem for my wife.

May 15th

I continue to hear whispering sounds. I now hear them along the landings, and I do not know how any sound from the speaking tubes could reach there. I have ventured to risk frightening my wife by asking her if she hears anything too, but she says she does not.

And always I hear them when I am alone.

I will confess that I am a little ruffled. Today as I was about to enter the drawing room, the sound came from along the corridor towards the back of the house, a hoarse sibilance seeming to snake towards me, and just as it stopped there was another sound like the scrape of a foot, as if someone were ducking out of sight. I turned quickly, my blood thumping, but the long space was quite empty, all the doors firmly shut.

I fear that I am of a sudden pushed by old age from my rational character. All of my life have I conducted myself with equanimity and reason. No vicissitude has ever knocked me from my senses – no storm at sea, no grief, not the deaths of two of my beloved children, nor the waywardness of my elder sons. That those sons should reject my very principles of rationality and align themselves with poets and dreamers and, like their mother, be happy to submit to the promptings of feeling and of imagined spirits, was indeed to me a matter of both puzzlement and chagrin. It is hard for a man who believes in a life of rigour – hard work, early rising, regular and healthy meals and a daily plunge in a cold bath – to countenance his sons lounging in their opium dens, wigless in the way that is now the fashion, their hair awry. Yet I reasoned that no good comes of quarrelling with one's children, and I took pains to accommodate them, so far even as to extend hospitality to their poet friends.

I think it may be said that I dealt fairly with my children, and with all whom I have encountered, which is a steadying thought to have in one's closing years.

No further sign of the light/shadow business to date.

May 17th

My discomposure continues.

A most odd happening when my wife and I were alone at dinner today. We enjoy the benefit of that modern invention, the dumb waiter, whereby food may be sent straight up to us from the kitchen without the need of human carrying. We are attacking our pudding today when a most prodigious sound of young girls giggling seems to burst from the shaft, and the cry, 'Look!' in a strange accent, as if some new maid, brought from other parts, were hollering up the hole. 'God's truth,' cries I to my wife, most annoyed that this contraption, designed not only to bring the food to us piping hot, but also to afford us a privacy hitherto unattainable in a house with servants, should allow such disruption of our peace. My wife looks at me blankly. Says I, 'Do you countenance such indiscretion by servants?' She wants to know of what indiscretion I speak. She has heard no giggling and no sound whatever.

Perhaps my wife is going deaf, I think, and I believe that she feared so too.

Yet tonight she tells me that no new maids have been employed, and that the cook when spoken to maintained that there were none in the kitchen at the time when we ate our pudding, one having been sent to the underground store for butter, the other outside for water.

My wife tells me, laughing: 'You have frightened the cook. She is afraid we are haunted.'

I laughed too, though I cannot claim that I felt at ease. My wife, whose fear of the supernatural has hitherto amused me, patted my arm in a matter-of-fact way and went to her withdrawing room.

I stepped out onto the landing. And then I thought I heard it again, fainter now, somewhere in the upper spaces of the house where no servants should be at that time, a voice calling, the words indistinguishable, and then a roiling of giggles, a trickling, bubbling sound.

Rain on the roof perhaps, I thought, that's all, but could not deny the broad sheet of sun lying on the pink stone of the stairs.

May 20th

I fear that I am now truly losing my reason.

Investigation of the system for channelling water from the roof to the tank on the lowest level has yielded no lack or fault likely to cause these unaccustomed sounds, which I have since heard yet again. My personal examination of the dumb waiter found no mechanism worn and no piece of crockery overlooked and rattling. Unless I am to succumb to a belief that ghosts walk this house, I must conclude that my eyes and ears have been deceiving me all along, and that this must extend to the shadows as well as sounds.

Today I looked up from my desk and thought I saw a man standing across the room. In an instant he was gone, and I knew him for what he was, a moment's vision, a dream, but what lasted in my mind was the gaze he seemed to beam towards me, a gaze of accusation.

Yet, just as I do not hold that any ghost has the capacity to rise up to reproach me, neither do I think that my conscience should do so. In all my dealings I have treated others with consideration. I did not disown my sons when they quarrelled with my philosophy; I even smuggled to safety one of their group in trouble for his radical activities. I made pains to understand and assuage my wife's sad longings, arranging her frequent journeys to the land of her birth. Our close servants have been treated as family, my man, a manumitted slave, enjoying many of the freedoms of any young English gentleman.

I should rather submit to the notion that we are haunted than to believe I am so far thrust from my reason as to imagine these presences. Yet what ghost would appear as these do, away from the traditional time of night and in the blare of the sun which flings itself in a gold river down our stairway and turning to diamonds the fine sugar on the table, substance of my trade?

May 21st

Not long since, this very evening, I suffered a most distressing vision. I had prepared to our bedroom to change for dinner. The maid had failed to pull the curtains and sun was filling the room, light glancing off the washstand and the pure white dimity bed frills dazzling my eyes. I went to the window to look down the valley, and experienced an alarming sensation. The view was quite changed: pale slabs of colour blocked the view of the river, as if films had formed before my eyes. I turned in. I felt blinded and giddy.

I heard voices I did not recognise on the landing.

I staggered rather than stepped into the dressing room and, though later I would find the room restored to its customary state, in that moment it appeared to me quite bare, bulging with sun and the curtains and furnishings and all gone.

Yet there in this dream, writ large on a plaque the wall, were my very own words, my instructions to the managers of my plantations that my slaves should be treated with humanity, that I would not suffer any human being committed by providence to my care to be treated with severity.

It is my eternal sadness that my abolitionist elder sons should have lumped me with those cruel plantation owners

who beat their slaves to death. It was nothing to my sons
in their blinkered idealism that when I inherited my first
plantation I freed the ill and starving slaves; they preferred
to point to the financial saving which this admittedly made,
along with the cheapness and investment of the child slaves I
replaced them with, and to the economic wisdom rather than
the philanthropy of providing my slaves with medical care
and clothes and land on which to grow crops of their own.
But humanity is surely not diminished by going hand in hand
with good economic sense. And humanity must be tempered
with justice, and the system maintained if our trade and the
prosperity of our land is to continue. If I told my managers
not to whip my slaves within hearing of abolitionist visitors,
then it were for the sake of harmony rather than the shame
my sons thought I should feel.

May 22nd

I see apparitions everywhere. They people the stairs and the
landings and hover at the entrance to rooms, and are such as
I never could imagine, in outlandish garb in colours of such
luminosity that, though I have lived in the brightness of the
West Indies, I did not know could exist. They gaze, they peer,
at my furnishings and contraptions. They must be ghosts after all, rather than my own projections, for they are alien,
and, though I cannot touch them, concrete-seeming, and I do
not know what connection they could have with the pictures
of black and broken skin now leaking through my mind . . .

WHAT MAY BE

POSSIBILITY

So you have reached the age of possibility.

You woke in the early hours. Morning crouched in blackness. The cat watched you with his wide unimpressed green eyes. Jake stirred as you left his side, giving off his faint yeasty smell. You fed the cat, you picked up your bags, ready-packed with your laptop and files, you stole out to the taxi and sped through London streets widened by emptiness, between buildings pulled back ready for the day. You caught the 6pm train. And here you are now tucked up in the seat you reserved, in the quiet carriage at the front of the train, the tilting Pendolino which will whip you in only just over two hours to your part-time post as a lecturer of Art, with a table for your laptop so you can put the finishing touches to your lecture, and facing the engine so when it starts to get light you can see the day opening up in the direction you're going.

You settle back, you take off your shoes.

You are thirty-one years old. You have made it, as far as anyone can make it, in this age of short-term contracts and the cult of the Next New Thing, and the consequent need to keep reinventing yourself. But then you're an artist, your stock-in-trade is invention, and because of who you are now you look on that as a stimulating challenge.

You are not the person you were. You see that person, that girl, as another, moving on a coloured screen you switch on sometimes just to compare: and there she is, unsure, she never really knew what she wanted to do, she thought it was English, she thought she'd be a writer, and at one time a musician. All those times she left her violin on the bus, the parachute of realization dropping around her as she stepped to the pavement and the bus pulled away. That was in the days when things and people gone from sight were out of touch, more or less, when you had to make efforts to contact them, when teenagers like you, like her, didn't have mobile phones. You'd have to go home to phone the depot, and Mum and Dad would be rolling their eyes, humorous but weary: a scatterbrain, a kook, that's what they'd got you down as, that was the character in which you thought you were trapped.

But you made it out of it, didn't you? Now you're a competent coper, here in an age when you simply press a button and, sitting in a London railway station, send the images to your students in Manchester, ready for the seminar today.

You get out your laptop.

A fortyish man in a pin-striped shirt takes the seat opposite, keying into his Blackberry.

OR:

You took your blue pin-striped shirt off the back of the door where you hung them when the girl brought them back in their silky plastic covers and collected the dirty ones. It's what you've been doing, having them cleaned professionally, since Jenny left with the kids. It's a cinch, no hassle, just the inconvenience of having to be in when she comes, and the ache in your chest when she shoves her short blonde hair behind her ear like that, which you know to squash, because you know it's only a rebound mechanism, and you're not sentimental: if there's one thing you can do in life, even when it comes to Jenny leaving, it's cope.

Let's face it, you despise anyone who can't.

And wouldn't you know it, the world is full of non-copers.

Like these jokers who run these trains. Last week: an hour late to your meeting in Manchester because some idiot forgot to get out of bed to drive the fucker you were booked on, and the chimpanzees in charge had no contingency plans for such an event. You can't believe it, or rather you can: no one thought that far ahead, or had the wit to conceive the contingency. A world of technology, of possibility, and all its potential wasted because it's in the hands of numbskulls and slackers.

And in the autumn: three hours late on account of a national joke, *leaves on the line*. And we're meant to swallow it, the idea that when for two whole centuries such flimsy organic matter was never any trouble, it stops today's modern trains in their tracks.

Here comes another non-coper: a bewildered-looking woman shrouded in Asian clothing, bundled onto the train by a smartly-dressed Asian man. You don't blame her, you're not that much of a bastard; even so, incompetence and inexperience are not things you like to look at for long.

You turn to your laptop, and the figures you'll be presenting in just over three hours' time.

OR:

You try to stop your heart thumping as Ahmed drives you through the dark early-morning streets. You're brave now, which is why you insisted on making this trip, you're in a brave new world where women travel alone. You've come so far already, alone by air to join Ahmed, though that was easier of course, with Ahmed waiting at the other end. This is more of an adventure, even though your cousin will meet you: you've never met him after all, or most of the cousins up there in the unknown damp north of this land.

You ought to be excited, and you are. Not afraid.

You've come so far already. You've learnt the language, you've even started to think in it. And you're someone, aren't you, the wife of a rich businessman, driven to the station in comfort, leaning back on plush leather, Ahmed's large hands lightly controlling the wheel. But that's the trouble: in a very short while he'll no longer be there, you'll be alone in a world where people see your jilaabah as a sign of repression, or simply strange and unwelcome and, with discomfort or distaste, look away.

Or is this the real trouble: the fact that you do after all need Ahmed in this way?

You hate these thoughts; they make a knot in your stomach. Best to quash them, concentrate on the practicalities, although of course Ahmed takes care of those: parking the car, quickly finding a trolley for your bag, marching you along the platform without any hesitation, right to the front of the train. So quickly, you hardly notice how he does it all, you miss the signs, the details passing you by so quickly that once you're left on your own you won't have the knowledge or experience to cope . . .

Ahmed stacks your case, settles you finally, and then he's going, he's gone and your heart empties out.

You catch the eyes of the two people with laptops on the other side of the aisle.

The young woman smiles but the man quickly looks away.

The train begins to move.

OR:

You ease the power lever, you pull the train out of the station and under the light-polluted sky. The monitor flickers, translating the signals transmitted to track-mounted receivers and picked up by the train's antennae.

Your stomach rumbles. You think of your kids still asleep as you left them, way to your left beneath the sulphur-coloured sky.

You're a meld of human and machine, at the nub of a vast sophisticated system, not long before it will be even vaster and more sophisticated, guided by satellites in the orange sky.

You're in control, but you also know that no system is infallible. There's always human error, and each technological innovation brings its new, often unimagined problems. Take leaves on the line: the new, previously unimagined speeds and weight of trains blasting the leaves into a carbonized coating which can cause the wheels to spin and fatally damage the lines. The unknown factor: it's remembering this which is part of your control.

The monitor flickers: clearance for tilting speed. You

slide the accelerator, the grey houses become fluid, the north-London suburb where your kids are still sleeping flicks by in an instant, turned invisible –

The cab around you explodes.

AND THEN:

You hear the bang, you hear – no feel – the wheels hit an object and then the screeching fills your ears, your brain, your every cavity and vein; you know it: the train is being derailed, you took your shoes off, the train is crashing and you'll need them, but you can't reach them, as the train goes on braking you're pushed forward over the table –

– you're pushed backwards, your back's to the engine, the safest place for a crash, but all to no avail because when the impact comes that woman across the table will come flying towards you, smash your skull –

– and the screaming inside you is the scream of the dreadful possibility which has always been inside you and which Ahmed never understood . . . and all the other, better possibilities are flying away from you, and Ahmed himself, his long face, his comfortable hands –

– Jake curled in the bed is flying away from you –

– your kids, their futures without you sealed now anyway forever, screaming off into the black impassive night.

The screaming stops. The train stops.

The lights go out, a missed heartbeat, a moment of blankness, and then the blinking fluorescence of emergency lights coming on.

There is silence, dead silence, as everyone adjusts to the fact: the train didn't crash. And then the murmurs begin, people asking each other what happened.

What *happened*. It's over, you think, adjusting your pinstriped collar: whatever happened, the safety system kicked in. Whatever it was, it didn't lead to calamity, to the end-stop which in those moments you thought was coming. You were wrong. To feel afraid was an error. Whatever happened was an error, overcome.

You tap your keyboard, the screen lights up again, the wi-fi kicks back, you get back to the true reality: your network, people you can influence, people who can help you, your own beautiful system.

The door behind you, the door leading to the cab, opens and someone bursts out, the train manager, and rushes down the carriage with an air of panic, unable presumably to take calmly a glitch in the system, in other words do his job; too preoccupied to answer the passengers attempting to ask him what happened – though no doubt in reality what happened isn't worth comment, and it's over, no point in fuelling the wide-eyed stress of the women – the Asian one across the aisle, leaning over to ask the one opposite you what's going on, pointlessly perpetuating a sense of drama, which although you're not sexist you have to say in your experience women do.

You get back to your figures.

You don't know, you tell the Asian woman.

The train has stopped with the first carriage, this carriage, just inside a suburban station, you can't tell which, there's no sign in sight.

The train manager comes back, making for the cab again; he's past before you can accost him and gone through the door. But a moment later he's back at a rush again, and this time you see his face: ashen white. You stand up in his path, you demand: *What's happened?*

He's trembling, his voice is shaking as he tells you: *We've hit a person.*

What? *What is it?* you ask the woman who spoke to the train manager. You can say this without having to think, you can think in the language now, but when she answers you can't make sense of the words, you just know that they're the leaking edges of the black pit you've been afraid of always and about which Ahmed has never guessed. The sense of the words settles at last, they form into concrete sounds and a terrifying picture: someone threw themselves off a bridge and landed on the cab.

You move over to the aisle seat, closer to the young English woman who is giving you these monumental words.

You stay in the aisle seat, you sense the Asian woman needs you to. Now someone's running on the platform with a torch, and off the end of the platform towards the carriages behind. You remember the judder of the wheels and the sound like a crunch. You feel sick. After a short while he comes back again, and the train manager comes back too, hurrying parallel inside the train, and disappears once more towards the cab.

Without warning, the lights go out again. Blackness, punctured by the wondering exclamations of people further down the carriage, people who wouldn't have heard what the train manager told you.

Your eyes begin to adjust: a weak light from the platform is infiltrating the darkness and picking out the guy opposite.

And you can't believe it, you can't *fucking believe it*: he's *still working on his laptop*.

He stops working though now, and gets out his phone.

You tell them in Manchester you won't be making the meeting now; *fatality on the line*. A phrase you hear so often it's hard to believe it's no less of an excuse than those leaves, and these guys running around like headless chickens have no experience of dealing with it, it seems.

And here's two more jokers, lit up in the doorway by a bundle of glo-sticks one of them is carrying: two young lads, catering staff, dithering before the door and making it open and shut and hover halfway, and whispering nervously: *Shall we do it now? . . . Yes! . . . What, now? . . . Yes, go on!* And one of them pushes the other into the compartment.

The one with the glo-sticks leans above you and places one in a bracket, and you can see your keyboard properly again.

↭

You can't believe it, you can't *fucking believe it*, but the guy opposite is tapping away at his laptop again.

One of the catering lads is carrying a box. He turns to the guy, hesitates, turns away again and catches your eye. Somewhere in the distance there's the wail of an ambulance siren, coming closer, and it hits you why it's dark again, why they would need to turn off the electricity, and just as the nausea threatens to overwhelm you the lad puts his hand in the box and brings something out and asks you: *D'you want a Twix?*

And then the ambulance arrives screaming, and in the darkness outside luminous jackets flicker, making their way down the outside of the train. Here inside they're still giving out the Twixes, but before they're halfway down the carriage the train manager comes in and announces they're evacuating the train.

You spin: *evacuating*, what does this word mean? You should know, you do yet you don't, you've lost your bearings and the words are spinning, you ask the English woman to be sure: *What did he say?*

You tell her, and she jumps up quickly, you know why, she wants to stay close, she's relying on you now, the one who thought to ask what happened, the coper, but you're not actually coping, you feel sick.

You put your laptop away smartly, you're in the front carriage and just in the station, which is lucky, but the others will be herded this way, so you'd better get off quick. You grab your coat and you're off, ready to be the first on whatever emergency transport they've laid on.

There's no emergency transport. The Asian woman sticks close as you question the station guard. He shrugs his shoulders: you'll need to go to Watford Junction. You ask him how. He tells you there's a bus stop outside the station.

People are pouring now from the front door of the train, soon the platform will be crowded and the sight will be hidden: the knot of luminous jackets crouched down beside the train. The Asian woman is asking, *What shall we do?* And you gather your wits, you realize you need to be quick to the bus stop, you avert your eyes from the huge dent in the cab, and lead her forward to the exit.

You can't believe it, you can't *fucking believe it*, that there's no system, nothing, to get people out of this situation, and nothing for the trauma beside a fucking tricksy box of Twix.

You get to the bus stop, and the man with the pin-striped shirt is there before you, talking on his phone.

They can't believe it in the Manchester office. You can believe it only too well, you tell them grimly, and put away your phone as others, headed by the two women, straggle up.

You struggle onto the bus with your case and the Englishwoman helps. You sit beside her all the way to Watford Junction, you follow her into the station, you stand close as you wait for the next train.

When it comes, the standard carriages are crowded.

Here, says the Englishwoman, rushing along the platform to first class. *But we don't have the tickets*, you protest as you catch up with her. *It's OK*, she insists, *they can't not let us, not after what's happened*, and she grabs at your bag and helps to heave it up.

You overtake the two women and hop into a different first-class carriage. And here you are, on course again. The day has closed back over the gruesome incident, the inconvenience has been minimized, the incompetence of railway management notwithstanding, and you'll only be an hour late for the meeting after all.

You've ended up in the first-class dining car. You're at a table with three others, and the Asian woman is once more seated across the aisle from you.

The waiter comes along the carriage, asking to see people's breakfast tickets.

You explain why you haven't got one.

He says, Well, he'll have to ask you to move.

You cry: *What?!!* You hear the way it comes out of you, a high-pitched squawk, which makes others around you jump, and turn and stare.

His face is impassive. No, he's sorry, but you don't have a ticket for breakfast, so he has to ask you to move.

And then you lose it. You've just got off a train where someone committed suicide, you've just been through an experience for which you ought have fucking counselling, leave alone a seat on a train, and he's quibbling about a *ticket*! And you're yelling this, the plug's been pulled on all the tension

88

and you're really yelling, and you're trembling, vibrating with anger and sorrow and all that old, old, fear of everything slipping out of control . . .

His face is a mask. He says he's sorry, you can stay in first class, but he really can't allow you to sit in the dining car.

He waits for you to stand.

Trembling, you do so.

Trembling, you move to the next carriage.

Through the window the horizon is now visible, tipping into view as the train tilts towards it on wide bend, and the sky above it is leaking open with a harsh naked light.

You can hear the guy with the pinstripes a few seats away, talking with ghoulish yet chirpy satisfaction on his phone.

You think of Jake, rising from the bed now and moving to his computer, and the image is a flat picture on a faraway screen . . .

You wait for the waiter to move you the way he moved the other young woman. He glances across at you. He looks away and bustles off. Something has stopped him, the fear of another harangue, perhaps, or maybe your clothes creating a barrier he didn't feel he could surmount.

You're here alone now, without her. You're on your own.

Well, you're safe, after all. All you have to do now is get out your phone – you've remembered your phone – because your cousin needs to know you'll be late. First of course you must ring Ahmed, you want to tell Ahmed, and Ahmed will want to know.

And he'll say he'll ring your cousin, he'll take over, he'll wrap you in the blanket of his competence and concern, and you'll relax and be glad yet, as always, you'll also resent re-laxing and being glad.

Your finger hovers above the button.

Through the window light is spreading rapidly over the moving plain.

You punch in your cousin's number instead.

There is no system for dealing with this: the sound of the explosion above your head replaying over and over, and the moment you knew it was a body, impacting with the huge metal machine of which you were the head, at a speed of one hundred and twenty miles per hour plus the rate at which it was falling, splitting the metal, opening up a black chasm which no counsellor sitting before you, no system in the world can breach, into which the horror of possibility will go on leaking forever . . . .

OR:

You step into the night and shut the door behind you.

But if only a door could shut it off, if closing your eyes could shut it off, her face when she told you, her upper lip coming down over her slightly protruding front tooth. That was what hooked you, that first time you met her, that expression: the spirit, the determination it revealed. You wanted that, you needed that, you wanted to be linked to it, absorbed in it, it was what you had been yearning for all your life. Then there it was, that determined drop of the lip, moving against you, shutting you off, shutting you into this permanent loop where the picture of it plays, along with the other pictures: her shoulder turning as she finally left, the time you saw her with the other, two figures, tauntingly bright, on a technicolor screen. All night long they unfold, these pictures, behind your lids, smearing sometimes like an old-fashioned film slipping a reel, but then with a judder, a sudden slump, the reel will recover, and you'll be forced to watch them again.

Night after night. No rest, the cells of your body ragged.

Out here, the night air holds the icy breath of their indifference; it is leaking from the stars.

No escape from it.

Except this single possibility: an arrow of purpose scouring the night towards you.

It scoops you up as you plunge towards it and out of the loop at last.

THE CHOICE CHAMBER

So HERE SHE is, in the kitchen with her two teenage sons. They're helping with the meal, and they're telling her about this Year 7 science experiment with maggots, which Sam did in school today.

'It's called The Choice Chamber,' Sam tells her, and she glances over at him chopping mushrooms, his big serious head on his slender neck, a little boy still, but beginning to metamorphose already, stuffing into himself each day new words and new knowledge, knowledge all of his own which he can impart to her. And there's Steve, grinning across at him, nodding and remembering three years back to his own Year 7, wide-shouldered – *huge*, which he likes to remind her by giving her a friendly tap on the head – a large blue vein standing out on his forearm like a proud tattoo, insignia of the adult maleness he's gone off to and comes back to her from.

Sam goes on, in the strangely formal diction he's adopted lately: 'You take a box and divide it up into several chambers. One large one, and four smaller ones leading off it but sealed off with doors. Each small chamber has a set of different conditions: damp and dark, damp and light, dry and dark, and dry and light. Each pupil in turn takes some maggots and places them in the large chamber and then removes the doors and observes which of the chambers, ie which set of conditions the maggots will be attracted to. The hypothesis is that that they'll make for the one with the damp and the dark, and the hypothesis was proved because everyone's did.'

'Except mine,' Steve says, and all three of them laugh at Steve's blind crazy maggots, which galloped off, against all expectation, into the dry and the light.

So here she is, in a kitchen, with teenaged children, her own, in this story of all the stories she ever imagined for herself: the one she most definitely decided against.

She was nineteen, a student in hall, the summer she so fiercely decided against it. There was a fashion that summer for headscarves tied gypsy-style: she tried it out and knocked on her best friend Jenna's door to show her, and Jenna said with delight and even jealousy: 'Ohmigod! You look like a bohemian *country mother*! I can just see you in some rambling farmhouse with an artist for a husband and loads of children running wild!'

She imagined it, she entered Jenna's fantasy; she made it her own: it blossomed around her, and yes, in that instant she longed for it, the grey stone of the farmhouse tucked between rolling hills, a lush wood behind the house with bluebells, the smell of oils coming from the barn converted to a studio, and those children: brown-limbed, tangle-haired, feral but fiercely intelligent and destined for their own artistic futures. And in the centre of it all herself, a figure of young and fecund motherhood, standing just as she was in that real moment in Jenna's doorway – older, of course, a few crows' feet, but just as slim and dressed the same in her jeans and sun-coloured top and the gold hoop earrings and the summery scarf tied at the back of her neck.

All before she focussed, came back to herself, her senses, and wondered what the hell she and Jenna were thinking: the husband the artist and her just a *mother*, a fate she'd be a total idiot to risk.

She whipped the scarf off sharpish; it was a fashion she never took to after all.

Yet here she is, in a farmhousey kitchen – albeit in a city sub-urb: it was the fashion when they did the house up, she and Angus, a fashion she did succumb to – the antique dresser and non-fitted pine cupboards, and the kids at the big old table, preparing an omelette while the saucepans simmer. And things changed, the world changed: she never did have to give up her career after all.

Steve stands to get the frying pan, and just as he does so the phone on the windowsill rings.

She goes to answer it. 'Hello?'

There's a brief silence, and then a woman's voice asks, 'Is that 7360?'

A voice she knows but can't place.

She says yes and there's another silence, it seems a shocked one.

At last the woman speaks again, aghast: 'Who is *that*?'

She says her name.

'Oh!' says the woman in horror, and puts the phone down.

'Who was it?' asks Steve, cracking the eggs, then holding the shell in mid-air, waiting because she hasn't replied.

❧

Jenna said she was crazy.

It was another summer, a very wet one. They had been graduated three years. They were living together in a top-floor flat in a suburb of the city. All night long the broken hod outside her window gurgled; going out in the morning to her job as a BBC researcher, she ran into soft wet billows. That summer she felt she had jumped and was swimming. All the world had gone fluid and all her possible courses, all her possible selves, were there in the liquid air for her to choose.

There was a boyfriend, a good-fun sort (apart from the fact that deep down, she knew, he just wanted to settle and have the 2.5 kids): he'd call on spec and suggest mad outings or turn up late at night with chips and beer and sit with them matily watching the late show. But she didn't want matey that summer, she didn't want that kind of comfort; in fact she didn't want a man at all, not necessarily, or just for sex, just for a flexing of her own gloriously, dangerously metamorphosing self. What she wanted was danger, her own dangerousness and no one else's.

Her dangerous self. That self which had flickered through adolescence – smoking in the playground, stealing from the store and legging it down the high street fuelled by the thrill of rebellion – that old self refocused to a higher purpose, swelling in the rain that summer and trying out the possible personae, clacking through the wet in killer heels or flitting in tomboy sneakers through the BBC doors.

She was happiest that summer when she was alone.

One day she strode into the BBC foyer to collect an artist, up from London to be interviewed.

He was slumped in the soft seat, a long frame in baggy jeans, eyes glaring from an angular face with a dangerousness that matched her own. She saw him see it, her don't-mess-with-me air; she saw him attracted to her in the instant, precisely because she was a challenge.

Ironic, really: it was this that hooked her.

It was the end of that summer, another wet evening, when she went to meet him from the train. As she crossed towards the station, light dissolved all around her in the wet dark, she had to dodge taxis emerging suddenly through waterfalls. There were holes in the station roof and water dripped on the tiles and went snaking across the floor.

She stood on the platform. Veils blew in from down the line where he would come. Then there were the lights of his train, sudden points in the swirling elements, homing in, bringing him with his dangerous exciting will, his utter focus on his art and on *sensual experience*, on booze and drugs and cigarettes, and now on her.

'You're crazy,' Jenna said, and yes she was, but crazy was what she wanted, none of that sensible half-life the boyfriend offered, though she had never gone so far as to send him away.

And the summer had progressed, and the garden swelled and the flower buds rotted unopened, and now, here at its end, her other lover came on the train to urge her once more to ditch the boyfriend and commit to his passionate self.

The train pulled in. The passengers began to unravel from the train. She didn't see him at first, and then he was upon her, and what she noticed was the whites of his eyes, glistening as if wet in the overhead lights, with a danger which for the first time she recognized as weakness, as need.

This was the moment she understood her real choice: between boredom or wreckage, between stability or passion.

⌖

Years after the choice was made she thought of the matey boyfriend she'd abandoned that summer. She knew where he was living, and somewhere she had his number.

In a moment of weakness she rang him, and was stunned when the voice that answered sounded like her own.

WHAT DO YOU DO IF

For Mary-Ann Coburn

WHAT DO YOU do if you're just going about your business – though truth to tell you don't have a lot of business: you're on your way back from yet another audition, and there you are walking through the corridor of something or nothing which the space between the buildings becomes after an audition, that slice of time when, depending on how you suited, your life might go one way or a completely different other – your heels clicking, you wore heels this time, and those pink glass earrings you picked up from a market, because you wanted to lend a touch of the character to your appearance, to let them see you as her – because that's what they need to be helped to do, some of these TV directors: they don't understand the actor's chameleon art (well, not many people understand it, you can lose a lover because he can't understand it: *How do I know you're not acting now?* he'll say, and at first you can laugh it off, sometimes even make it a game, above all take it as a compliment, but then there's the time, you've been making love, and he says it again, tracing his finger over the curve of your naked waist and hips, your real true self, and he isn't laughing, he's looking troubled) -

well, there you are now, clipping between the glassy walls of the city, still trailing something of the character you've just read for, and just as you come to a phone box the door bursts open and a girl almost throws herself into your arms?

'Please!' she says, in a foreign accent, holding out a phone card towards you.

Your instant instinct of course is to help. That's the point that too many people, including a lover, can fail to understand: that far from being a threat, a kind of deceit, your chameleon skill is based on empathy, the ability to put yourself in other people's shoes.

Right away you understand the situation. You take the young woman in: cheap clothes – anorak, tracksuit bottoms and trainers – scraped-back hair, flat pale face with an anxious expression; a young girl far from home, a foreign worker no doubt, newly arrived from some Eastern European village. And you put yourself in her shoes, her scuffed white trainers, and know how she'll feel: the unfamiliarity of it all, the slightly giddying sense of dislocation. You smile. You are reassuring. You take the phone card and say you'll show her how.

You see her visibly relax, her shoulders drop, yet there's still a tension about her as you hold the door and she goes before you into the phone box. You smile again your reassuring smile.

You look at the card. In fact, you've not used one yourself before. You peer at the instructions which clearly she's been unable to interpret. There's a code to be revealed by scratching, and she's done this already, but there's a number she has to ring first. You point to it, explanatory.

She nods, almost in irritation: she understands this, she is indicating. She says something in her Eastern European language and points from you to the buttons: she wants you to do it.

You get it now: it's the voice at the other end of the phone she can't follow.

You pick up the receiver and punch in the number. The computerised voice instructs you to key in the code. You press the buttons as she watches, crowding you now with the washing-powder smell of her clothes and something else not so pleasant, musty, sweaty, you're thinking, when the voice tells you the card has no credit remaining.

'No credit,' you tell her, putting down the receiver and shaking your head to try and make her understand. 'It's all used up.'

She shakes her own head in incomprehension.

'Finished!' you say. 'Finit! Empty!' She looks blank. You mime to explain. You point to the card then throw up your hands.

But still she doesn't understand, she shakes her head again, this time fiercely, and gestures for you to try again.

For a moment you feel almost bullied.

But you can make allowance, of course you can, for a young girl's anxiety in a big strange city, so you mime some more, you raise your arms in exaggerated illustration of use-lessness, you point again to the card and trace a nought with your finger in the air, you say, 'Kaput!'

At last she understands.

She swoops and grabs it off you, shockingly ferocious, and stares at it in disbelief.

And then she groans, her shoulders slump; she falls back against the glass, which strikes you as an oddly exaggerated gesture. She jags her hands in her pockets and pulls out the lining, dramatic, to show they are empty. And then she holds out her hand to you. Begging for cash.

This is the moment it comes to you that the whole thing has been a scam.

What do you do then? When it hits you that you got her wrong, that you weren't so good after all at getting inside her shoes. She was better at getting inside yours: at sizing up your sentimental mind of a middle-class Westerner afloat on the delusion that she can imagine herself in any situation, and thus ripe for being tricked by an illusion? *She's* the better actress, this girl in the anorak, slumped against the glass in apparent despair. And you, you've lost your grip on things now, your sense of your own insights, things are slipping. There's a smell in your mouth of confusion and corruption, the under-smell of this young woman which has sharpened, the smell, you think, of deceit.

And to stop the slipping you stand firm against the coercion.

You shake your head once more, but this time firmly in refusal. You make to push the door to usher her out, but it's awkward: somehow, without your noticing, she got herself between you and the door. And as you try to reach past her, she looks behind her, out through the glass – there's no doubt about this – she is looking for someone out there in the crowd. She must have an accomplice. And she's got you trapped there, standing between you and the door.

You're afraid now, but you're also angry. You hold tight

to your bag and you push forward roughly, push into her sweet-and-sour smell and past her, and get the door open.

She doesn't follow. You should go, stride off smartly into the crowd and away from this, which is not just a dodgy situation but a kind of abyss, a rent in your sense of things, but you're too curious not to look back.

She is slumped against the glass once more. She doesn't know you are watching. And as you watch her knees bend, give way, she slips down the glass to the piss-darkened floor, and you cannot doubt it: she is in despair.

Contrite, mortified even, you yank open the door, scrabble for your purse and grab a handful of change.

She has closed her eyes now. You bend and touch her on the shoulder and she opens them, slowly. Their look as she focuses on you is dead. You nudge your hand with the money towards her, and she turns her gaze slowly towards it.

She shakes her head.

'No, go on,' you say, 'take it!'

She ignores it. She gives a sigh that is almost a groan, and then heaves herself up and stands. She is looking out into the crowd now. There is no doubting it: she is expecting to see someone there.

'Take it!' you say, desperate now.

She shakes her head, she gives a deep shrug and pushes on the door and goes out.

What do you do then, as you watch her walk away between the jostling bodies, not running but slowly, her feet dragging, her whole body set in resignation, and the images tumble through your chameleon brain: the cramped journey at night across borders to the better life that had been promised, the house down the side street you were brought to, its grubby walls, the cheap partitions and the washing machine in the basement, the outside door with the intercom grille and the bell that goes all night long, the lock which was only once left undone, and the sudden understanding that there's no getting away after all, even kindly-looking women will stand in your way while the heavies scour the streets for a girl in scuffed white trainers, a fugitive's shoes?

FALLING

THEN ONE YEAR she started falling.

There were drinks (was she drunk? She doesn't think so), the dark glitter of many bottles on an island unit in a kitchen, architect-designed; ceiling lights dimmed, and sequins on the women's clothes catching the secret rays. An evening party in a festive season, in a capitalist Western city, black night beyond the front door and filtering off the still-cold coats in the hall. Silhouettes, and a young man's voice bemoaning the loss of a budget; another, from another corner, insisting best to sit tight, do nothing rash, see how things pan out, you never know. Voices fluttering like paper cut-outs, that's what she remembers, her sense of detachment – not a drunken detachment, she's sure, though who can ever be sure? She was distracted, certainly, she was wondering where her boyfriend had got to. She stepped out to the hallway to look for him, and into that moment, a long, long moment – this is how she remembers it – when she leaned her weight into her right high-heel and it slipped, pivoting, on a metal lip in the threshold. She felt herself turning, like a dancer, then tipping, and the moment was so slow that she could think about what was happening – detached she was, still – that there was nothing she could do to save herself, nothing she could hold onto, no one nearby to save her. Looking back on it afterwards she can see herself turning, tipping into a different future, and the moment itself as a pivot.

But of course also the moment was fast, which was another thing she was thinking, fully aware that there was just no time for any reflex in her body to stop her tipping. But then as she toppled, her reflexes did kick in: she careered forward in an effort to regain her balance, crouched and stamping, and she had the space to see the shocked faces of two people she was rushing towards at the end of the hall, one arrested in offering canapés to the other; she had an image in her head of the foolish, clumsy spectacle she must be making, and her all done up to make a different kind of impact in her cocktail dress with roses and her bright-red high heels. And then she hit the ground, the hard wooden floor of the hall, and all she remembers of that is the crashing sound of the wine glass in her left hand.

Next day she turned over what then happened: the men who'd been at the end of the hall crouching over her, concerned by the mess of blood and glass that was her hand. It riveted her too: the perpendicular embedded shards and the dark-red ribbons beginning to ooze. The way they helped her to her feet; she remembers the prodding sensation of their fingers in her armpits, the idiocy of her legs akimbo and exposing her pants as she tried to stand. It was her hand that was the dramatic thing, and it wasn't until next morning that she understood she'd hit the base of the doorpost with her head.

She was brushing her hair in her own hallway mirror: it wasn't easy because as well as damaging her hand and right knee she'd badly bruised her right shoulder. As the brush touched the side of her head she realized that even though she had slept without noticing it, her right ear was sore. She brought her hand up to feel her skull around it, and winced with pain.

In the mirror her boyfriend floated up behind her, pale, the way mirrors can make you, the slight asymmetry of his features reversed and exaggerated, the effect you get when you see others reflected. A man whom women found attractive, whom some woman last night had indeed found attractive, pulling him off to dance, which was where he'd been when she'd had her fall. And she voiced her thoughts to his reflection in the mirror: that an inch to the right and she'd have hit her head harder. She could have died.

And she turned to him, his real-life face, its asymmetry hardly visible, and it was obvious that he thought she was being melodramatic – well, he hadn't been there had he, he was removed from the vivid, concrete experience – but she didn't mind, because all that concerned her was how lucky she was to have had that one inch, to be in life now when she could be in death, and to make the most of it, not to fret about her boyfriend, not to let those trivial, personal worries so distract her she could go spinning off into a fall. And, since really it was the fault of the shoes she was wearing, never again to wear high heels.

But then she fell again.

She had once been a painter but had given it up for a more secure way of earning a living. After the fall, making the most of her life, deciding to do now what she was meant to be doing, she took up painting again. A year after the fall, near Christmas again, she was coming back from the studio and making for the shops. She strode in her jeans and trainers, a different, purposeful person now, no longer the hesitant woman she felt she had been. Late afternoon, and the navy-blue sky splintered by street-light decorations, darkness chipped into the gutter.

Ahead of her a pantechnicon came to rest on the narrow pavement outside the betting shop. The driver jumped out and nipped fast through the shop door – eager or desperate in these times of recession, or just because he'd parked illegally. He'd left no room on the pavement for pedestrians to pass. But she, striding in her jeans, proud to be as agile as the driver, stepped over the low wall he'd parked up to, a wall enclosing a narrow area in front of some abandoned shops. She cut along inside the wall, a dark corridor between the truck and the shop fronts, and reached the back of the lorry, where the low wall ended. She strode over the end of the wall and into an unenclosed corner. Her foot slipped in the slime of long-uncleared leaves; she fell headlong, out onto the pavement and right behind the truck.

It was fast this time; she knew nothing between the long slide of her foot and the impact with the ground. It was her knee she fell on, and the pain was so intense that for a moment or two she couldn't move. Then people were asking *Are you all right?*, a man with a briefcase stopping, slightly embarrassed, and then when she answered that she was and began struggling up, moving off into the road to get round the truck. A young woman with a pushchair who lingered longer, more worried, especially when, because the pain was so severe, she collapsed again briefly, but then finally too moving on, also forced into the road, looking back once to ask again *Are you sure you're all right?* before she disappeared around the truck.

She stood up. She walked a little way and turned. The driver shot out of the betting shop – hardly any time to place a bet, she'd have thought – and back into the cab.

Abandoning high heels had not saved her from falling. Losing her hesitancy hadn't saved her from falling. Indeed, it was her determination that had sent her plummeting, and maybe even the slippy soles of her trainers had made a contribution. What she needed after all was more care.

When it happened the next time she was wearing small heels again, pink ones to go with her dusky-pink jacket, but she was being careful. It was a summer evening this time; she was crossing the newly-paved square and looking to check that a tram wasn't coming. In the direction she was looking the tram lines gleamed on a flat white plane of paving stones; she didn't see that just where she was treading a kerb rose at an angle out of the flatness, and she tripped.

Again this time she had no experience of actually falling, but this time she seemed to hit the ground softly, there was something easy about it, something she was now used to doing, knew how to. She seemed to fall like an acrobat onto her hands, and she felt nothing, not the hardness of the paving, no pain, not until later when people rushed to help her, a young woman and a young man with a rucksack on one shoulder and a half-eaten kebab in his hand. *Are you all right?* they asked her, and the words echoed, a repetition, and then once again, as before, pain pierced the curtain of consciousness and her ankle racked her. And the thought came to her then that will never leave her now: that she was dreaming, is dreaming those falls, dreaming a life out of which she keeps falling.

That maybe, after that first time, she lies on a hospital bed, unconscious and dreaming.

Or that maybe this happened: she fell in a wooden hallway, and by the time the men with the canapés had reached her she had stopped breathing. And the party ended in disaster, blue lights revolving, slicing and scattering the discreet glamour.

Or: the truck driver, abandoning his bet in the worry about parking, dashed out of the betting shop, started up the engine and reversed to clear the low wall, right over the woman prone on the pavement behind . . .

Or maybe: the young man with the kebab watched as others tried to revive the woman in the pink jacket lying on the square. They pumped her chest and gave her the kiss of life, but though her eyes were wide open she wasn't breathing. She must have had a heart attack, somebody may have been saying. And now her face was turning blue. The young man dropped his kebab in horror. He had never seen a person die, and he didn't want to, he didn't know if this was what he was seeing. He wondered if he was dreaming.

WHERE THE STARLINGS FLY

Six months was all I spent in Brontë country.

At the start I was just in the city. Everything was supposed to be new and hopeful, I was newly married to a newly-qualified doctor, but through following Andy to his house job I'd ended up unemployed. And all around people kept dying.

We had married quarters, a ground-floor flat on a corner, close enough to the hospital for Andy to be on call for cardiac arrests, quite high up off the ground and looking out onto two different streets, so it felt floating and exposed. There was a door we didn't open, to a cellar with thick mould creeping up the stair walls. Two or three times a night, whenever Andy was on second call, the phone by the bed would slam into our sleep, and Andy would be up and into his trousers and legging it down the road. In the flat above was another young married houseman and sometimes they'd both be on call together, and as I pulled the covers back over I'd hear them running, two pairs of feet, a mad arrhythmia in the black night.

Sometimes the patients were saved, but more often, it seemed, they had gone before the doctors even got there. All around, it seemed, people's hearts were giving up, and no amount of massage and application of electrical equipment could make them struggle back into life, go on.

When Andy was on first call he slept in the hospital, and those nights on my own I gave a wide berth to the cellar, with its mould like an animal crouched flat against the wall behind the door.

The wife of the doctor upstairs was Danish. She was an Arts PhD, but like me she couldn't get a job. She had a thing about candles, and she even made her own. When we went up for drinks the room was lit by them entirely, tall spindles dripping, fat stubs stacked in complicated Danish holders, waxy ventricles pulsing. They made a great show of being happy, that couple, constantly praising and touching each other, but when they went to the kitchen the sound of them bickering haemorrhaged into the guttering room.

Finally I got a temporary job teaching English, eight miles away in Brontë country proper. It meant getting up at six to catch a bus to the other side of town, where I and another young female teacher would take a second bus to an isolated crossroads where the Head of Maths would pick us up in his car. He'd had a heart attack, the other female teacher told me, as we waited in the wind under a browning hill. 'But don't worry,' she said, laughing, 'I can drive, so if it happens again I can grab the wheel.' He didn't look as if he ought to have had suffered such a thing. He was tall, fortyish but with almost laughably baby-smooth skin, though the bright spots on his cheeks were a clue, I supposed. And though she'd been laughing when she said about grabbing the wheel, she always got in the front, and I, who couldn't drive, went in the back, and as we hurtled like a clot along the road between the hills, I'd have to suppress a feeling of imminent disaster.

I couldn't control the children. In teaching practice, in a direct-grant grammar school and a middle-class comprehensive, I'd been fine, but the things I'd learnt then – how to capture the children with a story, how to give things shape by organising them into themes, how to back it all up with visual aids – were lost on these kids from the scree of a council estate on a Yorkshire hill. They were small for their age, or fat; their hair was lank or dry bristles sticking up, as if damage had been laid down in their bodies already, and in spite of their mischievous behaviour, their eyes were most often expressionless and dull.

I was tired, I supposed, from the early starts and the interrupted nights.

My Head of Department tried to help me. He suggested getting the kids to make models with paper mâché, but when I did they slung the slimy grey stuff about the room. He gave me a tape recorder to focus their interest and they chose to ignore it, chasing each other round the tables instead. He was young for a Head of Department, twenty-nine. He had a curling reddish beard and a jolly, casual way with the kids that made my stomach clench, so far was it from my own inadequate teacher's manner.

Andy tried to talk me through it, but of course he had bigger things of his own: those moments, for instance, when, for the first time ever, his own pulse racing, he had to perform a life-or-death procedure, to avoid the mistake that would tip away the universe forever for someone.

Besides, with his shifts and my long days we weren't seeing each other very often.

Really, I knew, the kids sensed how I felt and took advantage.

☙

When I came back at night it was already dark and the starlings were on the city rooftops, a seething, sizzling mass. Where did they fly from? I wondered. Where did they go? Next morning of course the rooftops were silent; they'd gone, wheeling away in their strange formations. They went east, I supposed, to the farmlands on the Yorkshire plain, not the treeless hills where I headed each day.

Near the hospital, as I walked home, people passed in salwar kameez and saris, a population transported from a land of spices to a place of grey stone and heart-stopping cold, and artery-hardening fat and white bread.

Andy said: 'There's a body of evidence pointing to a link between depression and chemical imbalance in the brain.'

'But then,' he added, 'it's chicken and egg. Which is the cause and which the effect?'

He put his arms around me but, just at that moment, between our clamped chests his pager ruptured with alarm.

I had a wart on my index finger. I went with Andy to the doctors' rooms in the hospital, and one of the housemen got a phial of liquid nitrogen, and zapped the wart away with a swab like a magic wand. There were four of them there, Andy and three others, and they crowded, delighted, around my instantly wart-free finger. They were new enough doctors still to be thrilled by the miracles they found they could perform, as well as distraught about those they couldn't, but I could see they were already starting to get hardened. Only one of them was female, Blanka, a slight colourless girl whose father was Polish and whose mother was dead. She sat propped on the table laughing and all I could think of were bleak East European fields and exile and loss, and that, surely, when she tried to lift those patients grown huge and sclerotic, her tiny wrists would break.

One night when Andy was on first call, I stayed with the young female history teacher, who lived near the school and whose husband was away. She was an old-fashioned girl in stilettos and pencil skirts down past her knees and who carried a handbag over her arm, Jackie-Kennedy style. I was in awe of her, however: although so young she was a Deputy Head of Department, and had the power of calming the children with a look from her yellow-brown eyes. She was keen for me to stay, keen, it seemed, to show off her house; she'd been asking me for a while.

Next morning, after our companionable, rather boring evening, as we stood at the bus stop, her pale eyes filled with tears.

She said, 'I wish I could give up teaching.'

I was shocked. I'd always imagined that if you could control the children teaching would be joyous – indeed, I knew it for myself, though I'd practically forgotten it, from my teacher-training year.

'Oh yes,' she said. 'There's nothing I want more than to give it all up and be in my house with a baby all day.'

And I thought of her house, the place she saw as her haven

from whatever it was she needed to escape: an impermanent-looking box on a new estate scraped out of the side of a hill, its over-tidy hoovered rooms, the coldly laminate kitchen where we'd sat eating chops overcooked on her iceberg of a brand-new cooker and a chemically sweet pudding made out of powder from a packet.

All of a sudden, for no reason I could fathom, towards Christmas, the time of year that children as a rule are at their most restless, my classes settled down and started paying attention.

'I told you you'd do it,' said my Head of Department, leaning back with folded arms and an air of satisfaction.

Pete, his name was. I felt easier with him now.

I said, 'I think they got bored of fooling around.'

But really what I thought was in the end they took pity.

At Christmas flu hit the hospital.

They were on full emergency and Andy had to be there all the time. Those with clotted hearts or necrotising lungs or calloused livers were in especial danger, and perfectly healthy people were stuttering out of life with this swiftly lethal plague.

I got the flu myself – Andy, of course, had had the jab – and spent Christmas Day largely unconscious. One time I woke to the sense of skin, a white film over my eyes, which parted briefly to show me Andy's face leaning over: he'd got someone to cover and had rushed up the road to give me my present. The skin was closing again as he held up his gift: a pair of red sheepskin slippers he hadn't had time to wrap, and a net of oranges for vitamin C. I sank away into a world where the red slippers danced all on their own amongst oranges that rolled and skidded away.

By the time I'd recovered and the new term was start-ing, I'd lost a stone and there was snow on the ground. The first day at school it snowed again, fat flakes splatting down and swiftly covering the tracks dug across the playground. The electric light in the classrooms was greenish, the sound was muffled, and although I'd have thought the kids would be excited, they were subdued. At half-two it was decided to close the school early, but already by then, it turned out, the road down to the city was blocked, and those of us who lived there were marooned. I went back with Pete to spend the night on the sofa in the house he shared with an old university friend, out on the road towards Haworth, at the edge of town.

When we went to his car a lone child, a year-seven, was still in the playground. The snow was falling less solidly now, smaller flakes curling sideways and upwards, but the sky was a dark-grey overfull hammock. We went over to the child. He was wired with abandonment, his face screwed, but the moment he heard Pete's voice the lines of his body dropped with relief.

Next morning the school was still closed but the clouds had gone and the sky was a wide harsh realm of blue. Beyond Pete's kitchen window the hill rising to the moors was a blinding white plane, sparking nearby with rainbow light.

Pete came and stood beside me at the window.

He said, 'Pity you're leaving, now when you've got on top of it all.'

I had less than a month to go at the school. At the end of the month Andy's medical house job would end, and he'd start on the surgical one in Scotland. I'd already applied for a job in a Scottish school.

I thought of going to Scotland, and felt dreary.

I thought of not going. But where else would I go? Not back to my roots, where I'd been so unhappy.

I thought about that. I didn't like to think that something so past and irremediable could be the cause.

And then I wondered: had I married Andy, my healer husband, only to mend a chemical imbalance, to patch a hole in my soul that nobody could?

Pete said, 'The job's still yours, you know, if you want it,' and, tentative, moved closer and took hold of my elbow.

I considered moving out of his grasp. I considered staying quite still.

As I tried to decide, from beyond the brow of the hill a black cloud burst up into the blue: a huge flock of starlings. They wheeled over the stark hillside, away from their usual habitat, coming together, the cloud squeezing, teasing out in a loop then coming together again, writing their fluid message on the sky. And then they were gone, off behind the hill towards Haworth.

I thought of Haworth, which I'd always imagined but never been to.

I thought of the Brontës. I thought of them stitching their longings into homemade books, inking their losses into heart-healing stories.

I moved away, out of Pete's hand.

I knew how to make myself better. I knew what I'd do.

TIDES

OR

HOW STORIES DO OR
DON'T GET TOLD

THERE'S A SCENE that keeps coming back to me: the two of us standing at a wall by the sea one evening in Wales, me and him. It was dusk, the tide was out and just beginning to come in. It feels to me as if this moment is the focus of a story, our story, the point from which the tale could go backwards to all that happened before, and forwards, beyond that night. I see us from outside, silhouetted against the sea and the sky, me in my leather jacket, him in his waterproof – we'd been walking in the mountains – two figures in a tableau, the hero and the heroine of the narrative to be told.

But the light was fading, and as I stare into the memory the thing we were watching then is taking my attention now: the slip of sea coming in between the black and slick-shiny mud flats. The sky is fading, but this little river is paradoxically brightening, as if pulling all the light down into itself. It glistens like mercury, and even as we watch it's coming nearer and growing, because there on the straits the sea comes in quietly but fast from different directions at once.

And I can't yet see how to tell the story, or where to go from that moment, just the two of us together there at that wall by the sea.

I could pick the time he betrayed me, which would make the story a Gothic drama. It was autumn. The smell of rot was in the air and berries outside the window dripped like darkening blood. I wanted to lock him out for his betrayal, though his footstep on the path was like the footstep of the vampire to whom no door could be barred . . .

But I'm distracted from our story. Other stories are crowding me, the ones I was thinking of then by the sea, stories misty with legend and others concrete and linear with the building stones of history. My eye – then, and now in my memory – is drawn to the island across the water, black against the sky, plump with trees and the tales of the people who regarded them as sacred and there on that shore fought the Romans with hair and robes flying and torches flailing and blood-curdling cries. And nearer, drawn on the tide of that growing river, are the stories of the other invaders and travellers, the Celtic monks pulling onto the once-wooded shore where we stand, the Norman king who cut the trees down and built the castle looming behind us, setting the contours of Constantinople in the blue-green light of this north-western land.

Our figures, mine and his, are becoming indistinct to me in the dark.

And I'm thinking now, as I was thinking then, of the time in my childhood when I lived nearby, an English-speaking invader myself: my own story, which ended long before I met him, featuring custard made from powder and canings at school, and which can be a jovial realist tale or a misery memoir, depending on my mood.

It leads me on – stream-of-consciousness – to remember now that earlier that day we'd been shopping. He whizzed around with the trolley and I went straggling behind, side-tracked by the fact that the supermarket assistants spoke mostly in North-West English accents, not Welsh. Later on we made an inquiry in a shop that hadn't yet opened for business and was still being stocked with huge ugly soft toys by three Asian-looking guys. They were from our own town in England, I commented, but, surprised, they said no, they were locals, and when I asked them where they got their accents they said they had no idea.

And I stood in the pedestrianized High Street while he went to the bank machine, and watched a giant-seeming seagull drop onto a toy-town-seeming chimney, while a young mother, like my own mother here once, struggled by with a pushchair and kids, and I couldn't decide if it was a bad end to a story – a culture and a language swamped, in spite of the educational and heritage initiatives, by the Englishness sweeping down the new roads and the TV channels – or actually a good one, riddance of the differences that created old enmities.

Or maybe – more like – there's just no end to the story.

He came from the bank machine towards me, took my arm, waved back at the guys through the glass; we waved together, him and me: that's how we are now, a companionable couple, we went off for a companionable walk in the hills, it's not the heart-stopping thing it once was.

I could tell that story, the time I ended it between us. I could make it a feminist re-telling of a fairy tale: the waking princess (me) kicking the prince away from the glass coffin, ie my house which I had to myself again at last. I could end it there and people would be glad of a satisfying ending and none would be any the wiser, leaving out the way the house then filled with shadows, the fact that I stopped eating, that I longed for the sound of his step on the path again, and when it came, like a stroke on skin, rushed to the door and the light flooded in . . . And then I wouldn't be able to mention those years we spent together with the children – years like a TV sitcom – or indeed the two of us standing by the castle and the straits all that time later, side by side, not quite touching, watching the day dying, this image which just now seems central to it all.

The dark came down, the island was lost to us; the only thing to be seen was that river, still brightening and growing, and we turned into the pub under the castle wall just behind.

We'd bought a paper and tried to read it, but it was Saturday night and the pub was noisy and full. In spite of the bitter weather young women were wearing the briefest most glittery fashions and they shrieked with a confident abandon which within easy living memory would never have been allowed in this town. Young men bellowed. A lad nearby pulled his shirt from his trousers and kept showing off his belly and every now and then staggered like a toddler up to a fortyish guy sitting nearby and performed a low drunken bow.

Twenty today, that older chap explained, and then

engaged him, my companionable man, in conversation. I turned to the paper and read that the terrible summer had been caused by storms in the Arctic, which in turn had been caused by the warming of the seas elsewhere in the world. And then I looked back up and here in the pub it seemed the wrong story: the flowing drink, the skimpy clothes and bare flesh were the real and concrete components of a better-known, more comforting one, the certain progression of the familiar seasons.

My eye was caught by a teenage girl in the doorway, in a little-girl dress with puff sleeves and high princess waist, and I was swamped by nostalgia, which of course is what such fashions are designed to do to you, and I thought of myself in the time before I made all my choices, when all the narratives were open, when I couldn't have imagined I'd be sitting here one day with a man I almost lost, once because I nearly gave him up and once because he nearly died.

I could tell that last too, as a complete and rounded story, a grim, realist tale: the symbolic slam of the ambulance door, the ice-rink of the hospital corridor, his skull pushing up through his skin, the emergency operation. Would I mention my sense then that nothing had meaning and that my life after all was no story, or would I lie, since he recovered, and make those symbols fit a narrative arc with a happy ending?

I looked beyond him, and framed in the pub window was that channel of sea, now hugely swollen, still lit with a light that seemed to come from nowhere.

The other guy was still talking to him, in an accent part Welsh and part something else. He came from Liverpool, he was saying, and when he had kids here he vowed he'd bring them up properly Welsh. His son was the friend of that lad whose birthday it was; they were in the Welsh Guards, and the reason they were making hay this weekend was that the following week they were off to Afghanistan.

Outside the window the river broke an invisible barrier and poured across the mud flats.

The chap saw where I was looking. He said, did we know that the council sold the land on the harbour for a single penny to developers, to be rid of the responsibility of protecting the town when the sea level rises?

It was time to go. We picked up the paper.

Outside the sea had drowned the mud flats altogether and was lapping blackly, high against the wall.

The light was all gone.

We joined hands in the dark, in the oncoming rush of all the possible stories.

ACKNOWLEDGEMENTS

THANK YOU AGAIN to my publishers, Jen and Chris Hamilton-Emery, and thanks to the editors of the publications in which these stories were first published, and to the judges of the competitions in which some of them were placed.

The stories first appeared as follows:

'Used to Be', third prizewinner in the Carver competition 2008, and published in *Carve 2008*, a *Carve Magazine* anthology, 2011

'That Turbulent Stillness', published in *Red Room, New Short Stories Inspired by the Brontes*, ed. A J Ashworth (Unthank), 2013

'Looking for the Castle', runner-up (second prize) in the International Short Fiction Journal Prize 2014, and published in *Unthology 7*, ed. Ashley Stokes and Robin Jones (Unthank), 2015

'The Relentless Pull Of Gravity', published in *Stand Magazine*, Vol. 11 (2), 2012

'Clarrie and You', published in *Unthology 5*, ed. Ashley Stokes and Robin Jones (Unthank), 2014

'A Matter of Light', published in *The Wish Dog*, ed. Penny Thomas and Stephanie Tillotson (Honno), 2014

'Possibility', 'The Choice Chamber' and 'What Do You Do If', published in Salt Publishing's online magazine *Horizon Review*, 2008 & 2009

'Falling', shortlisted and highly commended in the Sean O'Faolain Competition 2010, and published in the online magazine *East of the Web*, 2013

'Where the Starlings Fly', published in the US in *Unbraiding the Short Story*, ed. Maurice A Lee (Createspace), 2014.

'Tides', published in the online magazine *The View From Here*, 2013, and in *Best British Short Stories 2014*, ed. Nicholas Royle (Salt), 2014

ALSO AVAILABLE FROM SALT

NEW FICTION FROM SALT

RON BUTLIN
Ghost Moon (978-1-907773-77-8)

KERRY HADLEY-PRYCE
The Black Country (978-1-78463-034-8)

IAN PARKINSON
The Beginning of the End (978-1-78463-026-3)

CHRISTOPHER PRENDERGAST
Septembers (978-1-907773-78-5)

JONATHAN TAYLOR
Melissa (978-1-78463-035-5)

GUY WARE
The Fat of Fed Beasts (978-1-78463-024-9)

MEIKE ZIERVOGEL
Kauther (978-1-78463-029-4)

MORE SHORT STORIES FROM SALT

BEST BRITISH SHORT STORIES

Best British Short Stories 2011 (978-1-907773-12-9),
edited by Nicholas Royle

Best British Short Stories 2012 (978-1-907773-18-1),
edited by Nicholas Royle

Best British Short Stories 2013 (978-1-907773-47-1),
edited by Nicholas Royle

Best British Short Stories 2014 (978-1-907773-67-9),
edited by Nicholas Royle

Best British Short Stories 2015 (978-1-78463-027-0),
edited by Nicholas Royle